INDIGO HAZE

Thug Love is the Best Love 3

AUBREÉ PYNN

B. Love Publications

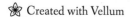 Created with Vellum

Introduction

Before you read –

Thank you for discovering Indie and Taj. If you haven't read parts 1 & 2 yet, I advise that you do before proceeding any further. This story picks up in the middle of the series. Also, keep in mind that there is one more installment after this and the book may not end the way you would like it to. However, I thank you for reading and sticking with me this far through this very emotional journey. Please try to keep any spoilers to a minimum.

Once again, I appreciate you.

- A.P.

Preface

The game is going to test you...never fold

Untitled

Open me and delete
All those nights I was weak
I gave up while you held it down
You're so hip but I know your hearts getting cold...
I can't lose you
-Mario: I Care for You

Chapter One

❧

Indigo "Indie" Sims

After a few hours, he slowly crept back to the house from the beach. Part of him hoped that everyone had left but Ajai and Ricky, but he knew better. Senior was probably pacing the porch, waiting for him to show back up so he could tell Indie a piece of his mind. And if Senior was still there, Malcolm was still there.

The brief thought of Malcolm made him groan hiss in annoyance. The second he laid eyes on him; his stomach turned. How the hell did Taj end up with someone like him? Indie could clearly see that this Malcolm guy was nothing like him and wasn't half of who he was. Nothing about him was real, the second he heard gunshots he would high tail it out of Crenshaw.

Shaking his head off of the thought of him, he switched gears and put his mind on Taj. Immediately, his chest tightened and began to ache. Although he said he was going to give her the space she needed to process, nothing about the idea of space settled him. If anything, it made him anxious to see her and explain himself. He had to. Taj was his girl then and she was his woman now. He just needed to get back into her space to speak his piece.

He finally made his way back to Mary's house and parked his mother's car in front of the house. For a few minutes, he sat in the car staring at the steering wheel and collecting his thoughts before walking back into the lion's den. Swinging his long legs out the car and shutting the door behind him, Indie made his way to the front door that was open with the metal screen door the only thing that stood between him and everyone inside.

"She's not answering the phone," Malcolm mumbled as Indie walked inside. The second Indie's foot hit the floor Malcolm snapped his head around and looked him up and down. "Why are you back here?"

Indie couldn't help but chuckle lightly while he ran his hand down his face. "I'm not one of them niggas in a suit your used to dealin' with... cool down before you get put down."

Senior chuckled and stroked the hairs in his salt and pepper goatee. "What are you going to do? Shoot him? I should have never let Baby anywhere near you."

"Chucky," Mary warned her brother from going further with any commentary that was bound to make the situation worse.

"And if I knew you would bring your hood ass back from Oakland, I would have damn sure made sure she was married before she laid her eyes on you again. What is it with you? Why can't you go the fuck away and leave my daughter alone?" Senior was starting to close the gap between him and Indie.

Indie clenched his jaw and stood his ground while Ricky stood up and waited just in case, he had to break them up.

"I didn't come back here to say shit to you. You don't have to like me, I'm cool on that. I got one concern..."

"It sure as hell ain't Ali. She's good, homeboy," Malcolm added, joining Senior in the pursuit to scare Indie but there wasn't any use. Indie wasn't going to back down from them.

"I handle niggas for a lot less and you think that you two scare me? Especially this *nigga?*" Indie questioned, pointing to Malcolm. "Goofy ass nigga."

"Oh yeah, I'll be goofy, but I got her...tagged and bagged," Malcolm snarled as though he had the hands to back up the shit he was talking to Indie.

Indigo's face flashed red before he balled his fists up at his sides. Ajai quickly jumped up and wedged herself between them. "This is enough. I'm sick of it. Indie, he ain't worth it. That's the type of funny ass nigga that'll press charges and cry to the police. We're not losing you again...we just got you back. Step back."

"Listen to shorty, Indie," Malcolm smirked like he won.

Indie stepped back and scratched his beard. "You are a bitch ass nigga. You might think you have her right now but that'll be short-lived."

"This is fucking ridiculous," Diane spoke up with agitation seeping through her tone. "Chucky get your ass out my son's face."

"I knew this had your name written all over it." Senior whipped his head around to snarl at Diane over his shoulder. "My daughter is too good for him. All he's going to do is knock her up and leave! She has a business she deserves someone who is going to add to her and not take away. You are trash."

"Chucky!" Mary shouted. "Fall back. You're dead ass wrong."

Indie's smirk crossed his face. Coolness laced in his smirk was the only thing keeping him from knocking Senior's lights out along with Malcolm's, who now took a step back but cheered Senior on like a cheerleader. "Ma, it's cool. He just wants what's best for Baby. We all do. This ain't about me though. It's all about him...blowing smoke to look like a dragon. He's a gecko. We know who you are and it's cool, Senior. You want your daughter to marry him for a bag, some security...but he's still standing here, instead of finding his *"girl"*. If you knew anything, you would know that I'm the bag, I'm the security and I'm that nigga she'll find her way back to. I don't have time to waste, I got shit to do and businesses to run. I'll be seeing you. Ma, let me take you home."

"Go do what you have to do. I'm going to see about Baby," Diane spoke up cutting Senior a mean side-eye.

"The hell you are!" Senior shouted, making Indie jump in his face. Ricky sprang toward the two and pried Indie away but there wasn't any use.

"Come on," Ajai scoffed. "Let's go find her."

As Mary, Diane, and Ajai walked out the door, Indie muttered something only him and Senior could hear. "I don't give a fuck who you are, talk to my mother like that again we're going to be doing more than exchanging words."

Stepping back and looking Malcolm up and down, he scoffed. "Fucking joke. Come on Ricky, we got shit to handle."

With one final glance, Indie walked out of the house and waited by Ricky's car. Once Ricky reached his car, he looked at Indie. "What the fuck, nigga? That's not what we talked about."

"Shit didn't go as planned," Indie replied, climbing inside the car.

Ricky settled behind the driver's seat and started the engine. "Did you at least catch up to her?"

"Nah, she got an Uber and ghosted me and then I got a call saying Joey got hooked up for making a deal," Indie massaged his temples and groaned. "Nobody fucking listens. I swear that shit fuckin' pisses me off."

"Did you go see him?"

Indie cut a look at Ricky, who knew better than to even ask the question in the first place. "I ain't stepping nowhere near county nigga, but I got Bobby on it. It'll be good."

"And what about Baby?"

Indie closed his eyes and ran his hand over his head. "I'll be seeing her. You know I don't stay away."

"Don't I know it."

TAJ ALI

EVERY SO OFTEN SHE WOULD LOOK OVER HER SHOULDER, hoping that Indie was somewhere behind trying to get her attention but after the third glance into the crowd of people, she let it go. Her mind was consumed. She was trying to find out why she was the last to know. Why would everyone hide this from her? She knew why Senior did what he did but Ricky and Aunt Mary? If anything, they should have said something.

The pain she felt was making her chest ache. The only thing she wanted to do was clear her head and then go home. The life she built with Malcolm wasn't as cozy as she felt in Crenshaw, but it was a lie that she was used to. A lie she lived with zero expectations and she knew what she was looking forward to day in and day out with him.

Checking into a hotel, she got her room key and made her way up to her floor. When she entered the room, she closed the door behind her, locked it and slid down the door to the floor. As long as Indie was dead, living the way she was made sense. It felt that was all she was going to get. That would be the closest thing she had. The closest thing she had to him. If anything, Malcolm was the furthest thing from Indie and he'd done nothing but solidified that.

She went from being hurt to being embarrassed, to being mad as hell, to feeling numb. It was emotions on repeat. Soon as one played out, another would come around and then bring a friend. Her mind flashed on how bad her depression was, how many nights of sleep she lost, and the PTSD of witnessing Bubba and Indie back-to-back caused. She was finally functioning and attempting to move on and here he was popping up, wanting to explain himself.

When she needed him, he was nowhere to be found. When she needed to be held no one was there. When she needed saving, she had to learn how to be her own hero. She had to navigate without her nurturer, her protector, her haven, her love, her heart. She moved around an empty vessel of nothing; incapable of loving and just trying to make the next day better than the previous.

But it was done, the decision was taken from her and they made it. They controlled the narrative. No one had anything to say to her. No one had anything to explain. Especially Senior. She silently vowed that this would be the last time someone let her down. This couldn't happen again.

Chapter Two

jai Carter

THEY DROVE AROUND TO FOUR HOTELS WHERE THEY thought that Taj would be. Taj wouldn't just run anywhere, she would always go somewhere she was comfortable, Ajai knew that. That's why she was so comfortable being back in Crenshaw although the memory was painful, initially.

"She can't be far," Mary hummed from the passenger seat as Ajai stared out the window. "Where could she be?"

Ajai closed her eyes and tried to replay their conversations from years ago. "Taj loves the beach. She has to be in Long Beach..."

Diane took the information and hoped that Taj was somewhere in Long Beach and not on the first thing smoking back to San Francisco. No one could fault her for her reaction. If anything, they were all wishing that they told her years ago, instead of waiting because Indie couldn't face the truth.

Almost forty minutes later, Diane was in Long Beach and Ajai was narrowing down the hotels. From the backseat, Ajai leaned up and pointed toward the Hyatt in front of them. "Let's see if she's there."

Up until now, they had no luck. The three of them stood at the reception desk of the hotel, hoping that the concierge would confirm that she was checked in. Ajai chewed the corner of her lip and bounced her leg while she watched the concierge peck away at her keyboard. It seemed like an eternity before the concierge looked up with a small smile. "She's here. Should I tell her that her family is here?"

Diane smiled and shook her head no. "We just want to surprise her. What's the room number?"

The concierge simply replied, "419."

Ajai took off toward the elevator, not really focused on what she was going to say to her. She just needed Taj to know that this wasn't meant to hurt her more. The trio stepped onto the elevator and looked around at each other.

"What do you say to someone who has had their heart broken time after time and then lied to on top of the heart-break? Does sorry really fix it?" Ajai asked, leaning on the wall reflecting about all four years.

Every year that passed, she loathed the fact that she and Taj weren't close. She loathed that she never reached out to see how she really was. She relied solely on Ricky to relay the ins and outs of Taj's wellbeing. Ajai realized now that Ricky kept Taj's feelings from her knowledge. Maybe it was because what he was telling Ajai was what he really wanted for Taj. To be happy, to move on, to find something that would make her forget about them.

Forget about Indie.

Forget about her.

Forget everything.

The dinging on the elevator doors opening, forced Ajai to step off behind Mary and Diane. Searching for the room, her heart started to beat harder and harder against its cage. Licking her dry lips, she stopped at the door and inhaled deeply. Raising her knuckles to knock them against the door, she exhaled and went through with the motion.

They waited silently, hearing her place her hands on the door, probably tiptoe to look through the peephole and scoff. "Taj, come on. I know you're mad at us. Just let us talk to you."

A faint chuckle came from behind the door before the locks turned and Taj yanked the door open. She stood on the other side with red rings around her swollen eyes. "You had four years to talk...now everyone wants to confess their sins...that's some good shit."

"Baby, let us in," Mary hummed, looking at Taj. It was visible to everyone how upset she was. But even still, she stepped back and let them in the room. "We didn't come to upset you anymore; we just want to talk."

"Talk about what?" Taj asked with her curls falling over her face. "You had four years to talk to me. And nobody said nothing. As far as I'm concerned...all y'all wasted my gotdamn time."

"Indie didn't want us to say anything," Ajai damn near pleaded for Taj to understand. "He didn't want to interrupt your life."

Taj's eyes flooded with tears again. She sucked her teeth, rolled her eyes and dared her tears to fall. "Fuck what Indie wanted. What about what I needed? Hm? What about that? Apparently, what I need is always put on the back burner and forgotten about."

"You know that's not true Baby. You're just upset," Mary spoke up.

Nothing they could say was going to satisfy Taj. "Upset? I am so far past upset. I'm fucking disgusted. With all of you."

"That's not fair, Taj," Ajai spoke up.

Taj snatched her head back and started walking toward Ajai. "FAIR? That's what we're doing now? We're going to talk about fair? Okay. Let's do it. Let's talk about. Let's talk about all the time I spent in counseling trying to be okay. Let's talk about screaming in my sleep because I can't get that night out of my head. Let's talk about grieving getting through the cycle and starting it all over again. Let's talk about not being able to move on because the man you gave your heart to, left! I fucking thought he was dead! No one understands that. I've been moving around here in love with a fucking ghost, only to find out he's alive and well! And everyone had a piece of him I mourned for. I mourned for him! For four years!! And y'all had him. Get out of my face with that bullshit! It's bullshit. I looked for him in everything... In a man, I can't even stand but I keep him around so I can –"

Taj stopped threw her hands up and shook her head. "I can't. I won't. I refuse. Get out."

"Baby," Mary spoke up once more, for Taj to shake her head no.

"If it didn't matter before. It doesn't matter right now. I'm good love."

They looked at each other and took turns sighing before walking out of the room. Ajai stopped and looked at her. "I am really sorry, Taj. I never meant to hurt you."

"No one ever means to hurt me."

Ajai didn't want to pull herself out of the room, it took everything she had to let the door close behind her and walk away. The only thing she could do at this point was to give Taj space enough to cool down. Once she was calm enough, they could revisit this conversation but not right now.

The ride back to Crenshaw was quiet and heavy. Everyone felt Taj's pain and Ajai couldn't take anything away from her. She was entitled to feel exactly how she felt but this situation was fucked up. Ajai watched her reaction to Indie and her heart broke into pieces.

Getting back to Crenshaw, Ajai got Bleu and headed home to find Ricky helping Indie with the remainder of the things he had left at the house, into his car. "Please tell me you aren't about to storm off and chase her."

Indie paused and slumped his shoulders. He simply replied, "Nah."

Ajai nodded her head and watched him come and in and out of the house with a troubled face and the energy to match. "Are you going to tell me what's wrong with you?"

"Besides the obvious? I'm moving into my own place got to make sure Joey has a place set up when he gets home. But chasing her down isn't off the table."

"Wait, what's going on with Joey?"

"He got hooked up for selling dope to an informant."

Chapter Three

T aj

AFTER A NIGHT OF SITTING IN HER EMOTIONS, TAJ decided to cut her trip short and return to San Francisco. At the least she just wanted to get away from all the emotion she felt while in Los Angeles. Her head was more clouded with noise and unsorted thoughts than it was before. But the grief was replaced with confusion; confusion fused itself into anger and her anger slowly brewing into a fire fueled by rage.

Walking into her condo without her luggage, she kicked the door shut. Taj shuffled over to the kitchen to grab a bottle of liquor and a bag of chips. She planned on finding a healthy series on Netflix to binge-watch and drown her troubles in the bottle. As she crossed her legs at the ankles on the ottoman, she untwisted the cap of the bottle and took it to the head. The burning of the dark liquor made her wince a bit. The burn of the Crown Royal didn't stop her from taking another gulp from the bottle.

Taj glanced down at her phone and let the notifications build up in her messages. Malcolm, Ricky, Ms. Diane, Auntie Mary, and Ajai, but nothing from her father. She chuckled and tossed her phone against the wall. Hoping that it shattered, she huffed and unrolled the bag of chips. Beginning her pity party session, she didn't move from her dent on the couch unless she needed to use the bathroom, get more snacks, or answer the door for her Door Dash delivery. In her drunken stupor, she dumped the contents of her purse and over-tipped the delivery guy. Food dropped on the white area rug, empty containers laid around the living room and it didn't bother her at all. When she was sober, she'd clean up after herself but right now she needed to let everything be what it was. A mess.

The sun set hours ago, and she was still watching the figures on the TV dance. The only sound outside of the dialogue from the show, was her talking back to the screen as though the actors could hear her. She talked and no one listened. No one heard her; they all just watched her drown in her unsorted emotion. It was sickening. With the cover pulled up to her neck she finally fell asleep for a few hours, only to be woken up by the sun peeking through the shades. Taj slowly stood to her feet and shuffled to the kitchen for a loaf of bread. Retrieving what she needed, she plopped back down in her spot and repeated the day over. The day turned into night and there was a fourth of liquor left in the new bottle.

Groaning and holding her head, Taj curled up, regretting the drunken state she lived in for almost three days. The turning of the knob was louder than the TV had been. The slam of it was even louder, making her squeeze her eyes shut and hum through the headache. She lifted her head off the arm of the chair and glanced over the cushion of the couch to see

Malcolm, parking her bags and his by the door. He visibly appeared to be worried about her but as he crept closer to her and observed the mess she made in a day and a half, the worry on his face was replaced by irritation.

"You had me looking all over the fucking hood and you were here?" he scoffed. Malcolm kicked an empty pizza box out his way over to her shattered phone on the other side of the room. "Really?"

Taj wanted to snap and ask him who the hell he thought he was talking to, but her head hurt too bad to go back and forth with him. "If you think I'm cleaning up this shit, you got another thing coming."

Through the pounding of her head, she chuckled softly but still didn't reply to him. "Is that my Don Julio 1942?"

Malcolm snatched the bottle he'd been saving for a special event from the end table and looked her over. "Are you serious right now?"

Pushing herself up from the couch, she stumbled toward the room to shower her pity and two-day funk away. The cold water would help her sober up to combat Malcolm. Right now, she felt that he had the upper hand to talk to her any way he wanted. The girl that would take it and retreat into her own little world was left in Los Angeles. She was over putting up with anyone else's shit for the sake of saying she was in a relationship, whether it was with Malcolm or her family. If they didn't care about the relationship, neither would she.

Jumping at the cold water beating against her body, she groaned and tensed up until her body adjusted to the temperature. With her hands placed on the stone wall of the shower, she rested her head against it and release the loud growl against it. Seeing Indie's face in her head, made her heart skip a beat and beat against her chest like it was trying to escape and get back to him. His touch brought back memories she held on to so tightly. To say that she would let him go now would be a lie. She knew that she would have to see him again and figure out the details but right now, she was lost, and her spirit was just as heavy as the glistening rock on her finger.

Taj stepped out of the shower and tightly wrapped the towel around her body as she dragged into the bedroom to find a pair of leggings and a t-shirt. After she was dressed, she slipped a pair of socks on her feet and traveled back to the living room, where Malcolm was standing in front of the window with his lips pressed together and the phone pressed to his ear. Her goal was to avoid the conversation about Indie as best as she could, but she knew that Malcolm was going to want to know what she knew. All she could do was tell him the truth and the truth was that she had no idea that the only man she loved, still had breath in his body.

Grabbing a trash bag from under the kitchen sink, she started cleaning up her mess while ear-hustling to Malcolm's phone conversation. "Ma, we're probably going to have to reschedule your visit."

Taj couldn't make out what his mother was saying but the look on his face said it all. He dropped his head, rubbed his forehead and cleared his throat. "I'll let you know when everything calms down. Don't worry about your ticket okay? I love you too. Bye."

Ending the call, he groaned before cutting his eyes over at Taj. "That was my mother...she was coming in to do a surprise engagement party for you, but I think it's best that she stays away until I figure out what I want."

Taj pushed her brows together and looked at him. "What do you mean, figure out what you want? You're either staying or leaving? What the fuck else is there to figure out?"

Malcolm laughed and turned around to face her. He crossed his arms over his chest and leaned on the beam the separated the massive windows. Taj stared at him staring back at her. She was looking to see if he were going to be as bold as he was in L.A. when he had an audience. "Here I am thinking that you were going home to close the door so we can move on, only to find out that your ex is living...you knew about this before we left?"

Taj tilted her head, trying to replay the events in her head to find out if she gave any indication that she knew Indie was still around. She chuckled and traced her bottom lip with the tip of her tongue. "That's what this is about?"

"You fucking right, that's what this is about. You in love a ghost of a nigga is one, you in love with a nigga that's back and trying to get you back, is another thing."

"Woah, we spend a day in Los Angeles, and you got some fucking bass in your voice now? Wow."

Taj resumed cleaning up her mess and let out a series of scoff, chuckles and *who does this nigga think he is* to herself. Failing to give him the answer he really wanted, prompted him to reach out from his posted position to grab her arm. It was tight enough to get her attention and set her off.

Taj's open palm met the side of his face, leaving a red mark on his mahogany-hued skin. His grip only tightened, and his face twisted as she glared at him. Taj mirrored his expression and snarled, "Don't you fucking grab me like you lost your mind."

"But that's what you like? Those hood niggas that handle you like this. I've done a lot of shit for you, Taj. I've taken a lot of shit from you. I've dealt with your coldness; your lack of affection toward me and boring-ass sex. I even tiptoed around this bitch so you would be comfortable. But what I'm not going to do is even play second best to some dirty ass hood ass nigga, who doesn't have half of what I have. You need to choose...me or him. It's not going to be both."

She yanked her arm away from him and pushed her hair out of her face. "If you think for a second that I will ever choose you over him, you're sadly mistaken. This is your chance to leave. I suggest you take it. Put your hands on me again and there will be no conversation."

Taj turned her back to him and finished cleaning up. Malcolm didn't move from his spot, instead, he watched her like she was under investigation. "Nigga lost his fucking mind trying to snatch me up. Malcolm if you want to fucking leave, leave."

"No," he growled. "I ain't going nowhere."

Chapter Four

Maria

Maria bounced through the office, hoping to hear some good news from Taj. She hoped that after a week of being off from work, she had time to reconnect with her family and close chapters that she left lingering open. She also wanted to give Taj and update on her relationship. Collecting the papers that required Taj's signature, Maria made her way into her office with a huge smile on her face. But the second she laid her eyes on Taj and the scowl that was on her face, she huffed and turned her smile down a few notches.

Placing the papers on the edge of the desk, Maria watched as Taj came to a stopping point to whatever it was that had her attention on her computer. Taj stopped and looked at Maria like Maria knew information and failed to give it to her. "Uh oh."

"When you talked to Ajai, what was the conversation?" Taj shot straight to the point. No hi, how are you? Or I like your shirt. "Run that past me again."

"Uh well," Maria cleared her throat and sat back in the seat. "She called and said that she missed you and she hated that she lost contact with you and that Senior wasn't taking his meds that he needed, and it would be great if you came home."

Taj raised her brows like she didn't believe her best friend. "That's all?"

"What is this all about?" Maria returned Taj's question with one of her own. "It sounds like you don't believe me...what happened?"

"Is that it, Maria?" Taj asked again.

"Yes, that's it. Why would there be something else, Taj?" Her voice was laced with a bit of aggravation toward the tone of Taj's voice. "What happened?"

Taj looked at Maria for a few moments and her face softened and her eyes dropped. Maria got up to close the door before they continued their conversation. Taj looked at her hands and inhaled before looking back up. "Well, I got home. Everything felt fine, I wasn't overwhelmed. Malcolm was off the handle but that's another conversation for another day. Everything was fine, everyone was laughing and talking and getting along and..."

"And what?" Maria asked anxious to get the bottom of Taj's attitude.

"Ms. Diane walks in and coming in right behind her was Indigo," Taj released, looking back down at her tattoo and her engagement ring.

Maria gasped and covered her mouth. Her eyes were big as she tried to process the information. "Taj Ali, do not play with me. None of that shit is funny."

"Yeah, well how do you think I feel right now?" Taj mumbled and bit her trembling lip.

Maria fell back in her seat and exhaled. "Wow, this is a lot. I don't understand...how?"

Taj shrugged her shoulders. "I don't know."

"Wait, you didn't talk to him?"

"No, I freaked the fuck out and left."

"Taj..."

Taj looked at her and shrugged her shoulders. "What?"

"After four years of going through everything you went through, you didn't even ask how? Or why?"

Taj shook her head. "Not really. I was really in shock...I want to know but I don't know if I can handle seeing him again."

"You can't handle seeing the man you lost, again? Does this have anything to do with Malcolm? I'm sure he acted a black ass fool."

Instantly Taj rolled her eyes. "That's an understatement. He was a bitch from the time we got there up until the time I left him there."

Maria couldn't help but laugh at the last comment. "You left him in Crenshaw."

Taj poked her lip out and nodded her head. "I sure as hell did. He was tripping over stray bullets, hotels, what I was wearing, my ring and of course he tried to get into it with Indie."

"This sounds like a mess."

"Because it is a mess. It's a big mess and I'm in the middle trying to sort through it... what do you do? I'm somewhere between wanting to run back to him and actually killing him for putting me through this. But the shit that trips me up and it's really fucking with me, is that everyone knew but me."

Maria threw her hands up in surrender. "I had no clue. If I

did, I would have gone with you instead of your fiancé and made you talk to him...how's everything at the house?"

Taj looked at Maria and pressed her lips together. "Malcolm is out his fucking mind...you know what he told me? I needed to choose him over Indie."

"Can we just throw him away already?" Maria huffed and rubbed her temples. "I'm really getting sick of him and I don't have to live with him."

Taj pressed her lips together and rolled her eyes after replying, "I don't know what to do. I don't know how to feel, how to react, what to say. But I know that Senior knew for four years and didn't tell me shit. I'm mad with Indie, there's no debate there, but I am livid with Senior. Like if I never see him again, it will be too soon."

"Oh shit," Maria groaned. "You know that's not good."

"I understand that." Taj licked her lips and hummed. "I'm sorry for coming at you crazy."

"Don't even mention it... I get it now. You know I got your back with whatever you decide to do. But right now, the priority on the list is to talk to Indie and hear everything he has to say. This has to be hard for him too. I highly doubt that he could get to you before now, he would have."

"You think? I don't think so..."

Maria stood up and sighed. "Sometimes men process shit different. Just be open to it when the time comes. I hope he won't wait any longer though."

"Yeah, me neither," Taj muttered before Maria winked and blew a kiss in her direction.

Returning back to her office, Maria dropped in her seat and groaned, "What a mess."

"Hey Maria," the admin spoke up, tapping her knuckles on the door. "We just got another request for a grant. Ali's door was closed, I don't know if she wanted it or..."

"Who is it from?"

"Indigo Sims."

Maria's eyes shot open. "I'll take it. Thank you."

She waited for the admin to leave to look at the request for the grant. Reading the description of the reason why they were requesting the grant, Maria hummed to herself and grabbed her phone out her top drawer. "If I wait on them to talk it'll be another four years."

Untitled

For most men, these hoes are a dream come true
But a dream girl is the girl that dreams of you
I got everything I need, all I want is you
That's why a nigga still cuffin' when the seasons through
All I want is you.
Chris Brown: All I Want

Chapter Five

✿

J oey

A WEEK IN JAIL WAS GOING EXACTLY HOW HE IMAGINED IT would. The food sucked and the living conditions weren't close to what he was used to. However, he held his head high and took whatever came his way. After all, the only one he had to blame for being there was himself and had to eat the meal he prepared for himself.

Running his hand over his head, he groaned and waited on the line for the phones to get clear so he could call Indie. Joey still hadn't built up the courage to call his mother. He didn't want to see that disappointment rested in the lines on her face and he sure didn't want to hear it in her voice.

Scanning the area, he scoffed softly to himself. The gang culture outside the county walls was just the same, if not worse inside. He had to keep his head leveled and remember how Indie handled situations. There were a lot of niggas he had to pass, who either shot at him or he shot at. His head was on a swivel just in case anyone wanted to roll up on him.

Before he could get too deep into his paranoia, the officer snapped his fingers at him and directed him to an empty phone. "You got fifteen minutes Sims!"

Joey inhaled and stepped forward. After dialing Indie's number, he waited anxiously for him to pick up. Right before the phone was connected to voicemail, Indie picked up. "What up, nigga?"

Joey let out a sigh of relief before, letting a tiny smile turn the corners of his mouth upward. "How you been? You good?"

"I need to be asking you that. I'm gonna be how I'm gonna be. How's everything in there? Ain't nobody trying you?"

"Nah, a few crazy looks here and there but ain't much to talk about. You need to give me the rundown," Joey started. He knew that Indie knew exactly what he was talking about. "What's going on with my girl?"

The nervous chuckle Indie released on the other end of the phone let Joey know that there absolutely something going on. "Nigga...this ain't about me. You met with Bobby?"

"Yeah, and you know what he said so stop playing with me." Joey scoffed, not letting Indie off the hook too easily. "I know she's pissed."

"My nigga beyond...she straight ghosted me," Indie groaned. "I don't know how to even get that shit back on track, that's a whole new woman."

"Yeah, so?" Joey shrugged his shoulders and waited for another excuse. "Kings don't make no fucking excuses. Own that shit, you fucked up. I gave you an in, go take it and get your girl. When I come home, I want to see her, make that shit happen."

Indie grew silent so Joey switched subjects. He knew his brother was harder on himself more than he was on anyone else. He didn't like when anyone else called him on his shit. Up until now, Indie had been on it and hadn't missed a beat.

"How's the business? We got buildings?" Joey asked, turning around to look around.

"Everything is cool. Ricky and I are going to look at everything in a couple of days. Thank you for looking out." Indigo's words went a lot more to Joey than he knew. Since Joey was a little boy, he looked up to Indie. Everything Indie did, Joey wanted to do, the good and the bad. It was just the way it had always been.

Palming his face, Joey hummed and nodded as if Indie could see him. "Don't mention it. It's the least I could do."

"Ay, look. You'll be doing more than just this. I need you to keep your head and don't get in any shit. Bobby has been working his ass off to get you out. When you get home no more of this shit, aight?"

Joey nodded again. "You got it."

"Sims! Hand it up, you got a visitor!" the officer shouted in his direction, making Joey nod his head in his direction indicated he heard him and was getting ready to wrap up his call.

"Aye, make sure you actually listen to me, aight? I'll call you on Sunday."

"You good? You need any more commissary or anything?"

"Nah, my books are still good. Just handle all the shit you need to. I'm cool," Joey confirmed once more before they said their goodbyes and disconnected. Stepping away from the phones, Joey stood on the line, held his wrists out to be cuffed and escorted down the hall into the visitation area. He was expecting to see Bobby but instead, it was his mother.

His head dropped and started to turn to the office. The officer shook his head, no. "You're going to talk to your mother.

She's been through hell with both of you. You owe her this much."

Joey raised his brow as the officer chuckled and took the cuffs off of him. "Oh yeah, we know all about the Sims boys. Y'all are urban legends. Everyone wants to be y'all. Why do you think no one has tried to touch you in here? Your brother's reputation precedes you. I heard you are wild as hell but Indie...he has a lot to teach you."

Joey licked his dry lips and nodded his head. "Appreciate it."

"It's nothing, go talk to your mama."

Pushing himself further into the room, he made his way over to his mother and sat across from her. Surprisingly, Diane didn't look as upset as Joey thought she would be.

"Hey ma," Joey muttered, looking as she nodded her head. "I've been meaning to call."

"No, you haven't," she replied, shutting him down. "You called your brother though and I understand why. You gotta get your shit together. I've always turned a blind eye to the shit you and your brother did because it was damn near impossible for you two not to get caught up in it. Every man in my family was involved in that shit and then I met your father and I swore that our lives would be different, and it was for a while. But then it went right back to shit. I will not be doing this again. I will not pretend to bury a son and have him come home a shell of who he was. I will not lose any more sleep over a son that chooses to be a street nigga when the world is at his fingertips. Joey, you are so much more than this. When you get home, this shit is done. Are we clear?"

"Yeah, ma. We clear," Joey spoke up, looking at the stern-ness in his mother's face.

"Good, I have to go to work. I've talked to Bobby and he

said you'll be home soon. Stay out of trouble. I love you, Joseph."

"I love you too, Ma."

"Words versus actions. You two aren't about to kill me." Diane waved her finger and stood up. Joey followed suit and wrapped his mother in his arms. Kissing her cheek, he quickly released her before the officers tackled him. "I'll see you soon."

Chapter Six

R icky

"WHY THE FUCK ARE YOU SO QUIET?" INDIE GROANED
from the passenger seat with his chin resting between his
knuckles and his thumb. Ricky chuckled at Indie's rumble and
continued down the street towards the bank.

The legit business was picking up, and Ricky had his hands
full making sure that everything was going smoothly. Even
though Indie made it clear that they were done with the streets
after the last of everything was sold, Ricky still had his hand in
the mix. He wanted to make sure that the money that they were
spending wouldn't run dry. Ricky knew that if Indie caught
wind that he was still in the mix, he would hit the roof, so he
made sure to be extra careful with the way he moved. He didn't
even tell Manny what he was up to.

Indie turned his head slightly to look at him, "What's funny?"

"You nigga," Ricky shared. "You got a lot of shit going on and you're internalizing that shit again."

"What the fuck else am I supposed to do?"

"Talk. You're going to give yourself a fuckin' stroke."

Indie groaned and ran his hand down his face and sunk further into the seat. With his hand running over his jeans. "I got that feeling that shit ain't about to go the way I want it to go."

Ricky sighed and gripped the steering wheel. "That's because you ain't livin' right, nigga. Look, it's been damn near two weeks since everything blew up in your face. How many of us got to tell you to stop being a bitch and take your ass kickin' like a man? She's going to be pissed off. It is what it is. She ain't answering none of our calls. You're going to wait another four years? Let her marry that bum ass nigga?"

Indie scoffed like the idea was completely asinine, but Ricky knew the longer he waited to fix things between him and Taj, the harder it would be to repair it. She was only going to wait so much longer for him. "She ain't going to marry that weirdo."

"Oh, you don't think so? I know you saw that ring just like I did. You got to face it; players fuck up too but there has never been anything you fucked up that you didn't fix."

Ricky was fed up with the stagnant area Indie found himself in. Yeah, he made moves but none of the moves was making him happy. He knew that Indie could successfully be a legit businessman and hate it, the same way he hated being a successful street nigga. Everything Indie was to better everyone around him, although he claimed that it was for him too, Ricky knew that Indie would never be complete until he had his rib back.

"You need her. That's just how that goes. I watched her grieve over you, year after year. It broke my heart. I need you to get your shit together. Shit will never go right until you do right by her. A man ain't complete without his rib."

"I hear you...I just don't know where to fuckin' start."

"You got the keys to every damn city you step foot in. You know where to start. You have never had a problem pulling up on nobody and now you playing bitch, nigga. I'm telling you this, I'm not going to be looking at your sad ass face too much longer. I can't take it," Ricky rumbled, pulling into the parking lot of the bank.

"I don't have a sad face; this is my face."

"You lie. You know you miss her. Just get it together, she don't love nothing about that nigga she's with."

"Oh yeah, why is she with him then?" Indie scoffed in envy.

Ricky kissed his teeth and swung the door of the car open, "Because the nigga she loves is being a lil' bitch and playing like he ain't never pulled up on nobody before."

"Call me a bitch again and see if I don't yoke your ass up."

"I'd love to see it." Ricky killed the engine and met Indie at the trunk to grab a duffle bag of cash.

"Where the fuck you get that?" Indie questioned, looking at him oddly.

Ricky laughed it off and waited for Indie to grab his duffle bag to shut the trunk. "I had some extra."

"You had some extra?" he questioned Ricky. "You fuckin' with me?"

"Nah, I don't like your ass that much to be fuckin' with you," Ricky shot.

Indie pulled himself away from the car and mumbled so only the two of them could hear, "You better not be. I said the last shipment was the last. You're not about to get me fucked up out here."

"Yo, you're buggin'."

"Ain't nobody buggin', nigga. I'm not going back to jail over no dumb shit. Give me your word you ain't."

Ricky huffed and looked Indie up and down. "I told you I wasn't, let that be enough. If not, I'm leaving your ass here and I'm going the fuck home with my money."

"Highly fuckin' unlikely."

"What was that?"

Indie turned to face him and clenched his jaw. "We got heat on us, nigga. They're looking for a reason to wrap us all up. They got Joey thinking if they leave him hangin' in the wind and pile his charges, he's going to talk. I am not getting caught up with this shit. I know you're fucking up to something. Shut it down."

Ricky stepped around Indie and walked away toward the bank. "I said what I said."

"Aight," Indie grunted, nodding his head and putting his attitude to the side. "Aight."

Ricky strolled into the bank and ignored anything else that Indie could mutter behind him. The best thing for him to do was to deflect Indie as much as he could, until he was ready to stop. Indie was a bone with a bone when it came down to making sure that everyone stayed the course. Ricky felt that he was going to bring this up again and he needed to be ready for it next. He would hope that Indie would distract himself with Taj enough, not to worry about what he was doing.

Chapter Seven

T aj

"I AM NOT ANSWERING THAT," TAJ MUMBLED TO HERSELF, hearing a knock on the door. "I didn't invite anyone and everyone who belongs in this house has a key. Unfortunately."

Taking a slow sip of her tea, Taj sunk into the seat happy to have some peace and quiet after a long day at work. For that last few days, she'd been confined to her own bubble where there was nothing but peace. The fact that Malcolm was out of town on business helped her clear her head and decompress. She needed to find a way to get Malcolm out of her hair without triggering him. It seemed that the more things started to happen, and ghosts started turning up, he became more and more irate. The Malcolm Taj thought she had in her space, was not the man that had been rearing his ugly head. She knew it had a lot to do with Indie but he either had to get with it or get lost.

The steady knock at the door continued while Taj continued to steadily ignore it. Well, as long as it was a pleasant knock, she paid it no mind at all. Instead of watching Netflix, she hit the button for the surround sound and let Tupac play. Bopping her head to the music blasting out the speakers and sitting on the couch, her mind faced back to Indie. This was his go-to song when they would ride around the city with her feet on the dash.

How do you want it? How do you feel? Growing up as a nigga in the cash game. I'm livin' in the fast lane, I'm for real.

Just as fast as she almost slipped back into the thoughts of Indie she was overtaken by anger, remembering his weak pleas for her to hear him out. The thought alone pissed her off again making her turn the music off and run her hand over her face, vigorously trying to rid herself of feelings. She couldn't. Up until now, she'd done a great job of shutting her feelings down. If she knew that all it would take was two days and a four-year-old lie to come to the light, she would have stayed her unhappy ass at home. Taj has lived in the bubble of her unhappiness for years, now everything she thought she knew was making her question every move she made from then, all the way up until now.

Caught up in her thoughts, she forgot that someone had steadily been knocking. It wasn't until it became a full-blown bang against her door that she couldn't drown it out anymore, that made her growl deeply at the persistence. Placing her teacup on the end table, she jolted from the couch to go see who had lost their minds. "Whoever the hell this is better have a good fuckin' reason they're bangin' on my door like I owe them money."

She hiked herself to her tiptoes and peeked out the hole on the steel door.

The sight of the person on the other side made her growl again, this time louder and deeper and more laced with agitation. How dare he pop-up here and interrupt her peacefulness? Taj was inclined to leave his ass on the other side of the door banging until his hands couldn't open but she knew if she did, he would only stay out there all night until someone called security on him.

Yanking the door open, she snarled at him. Before asking him any questions, she glared at him from the sorry ass expression on his face to the Nike jogging suit he found himself wearing. Blocking the doorway so he couldn't walk in and settle into the little piece of peace she had left, Taj asked, "Why are you here? I thought I made myself very clear about you being involved in anything I have going on."

"Baby," Senior hummed. As irritated as he wanted to be with her attitude, he understood where this anger came from. Although things between the two of them were strained, he was happy to see her. However, he was bracing for impact. "Why haven't you been answering the phone? I've been calling since I left L.A."

Taj scoffed, rolled her eyes and stomped back to her seat on the couch. "First of all, Charles, you could have stayed there. I really hate you wasting your money on my account. Second of all, I blocked your number and yet here you are...standing in my house."

Senior dropped his head, put a hand on his hip and pinched the bridge of his nose. With a sigh, he released, "Taj Ali Adams."

"Charles Senior," Taj countered while placing her hands on her hips. "Why are you here? You're wasting my time."

Senior huffed, dropped his hands his side and traveled over

the island in the middle of the kitchen. "Okay, why are you mad? Because I didn't tell you your little boyfriend was alive?"

She snorted in laughter that reverberated off the walls, the windows, and anything that filled the open floor plan of her home. Instantly, she wished that instead of drinking green tea and trying to find her center, she opted for alcohol. "That comment... you really don't get it. You don't fucking get it. You lied to me..."

"It was for your own good," Senior defended, causing Taj to scoff and roll her eyes. "You're not a parent Taj. You don't get it."

"I don't have to be a parent to get it. And you don't have to be me to understand that I lost three times. Mom, then Bubba, and then Indie, or so I thought. You didn't have to watch Bubba die; you didn't feel what it felt like to hold him and watch him fight to hang on and lose. And you damn sure weren't in that car with me when they sprayed it with bullets. If anything, he saved my life, not because he had to but because he loved me." Taj had tears in her eyes that threatened to spill over and just as she was about to lose it, Malcolm walked through the door. If wasn't already irritated, she was now. The sight of the two of them standing there, made her push her hands in her hair and scratch her scalp and groaned deeply.

"You got to be kiddin' me. Not both of them at the same time."

"Am I interrupting something?" Malcolm asked, bouncing his eyes from Taj to Senior. "Everything ok?"

"Oh, now you want to act like you care?" Taj spat in Malcolm's direction, making a grimace grace his face before Senior looked at him. Malcolm quickly straightened his face, loosened his tie and cleared his throat.

Senior ignored Taj's comment and turned to Malcolm and outstretched his hand for Malcolm to shake. "I just wanted to come and check on Taj. See how she was doing after...you know."

Malcolm cut his eyes at Taj as she folded her arms across her chest, daring Malcolm to say something slick. As the hours passed through the day, she became less and less willing to deal with his bullshit and his bullshit attitude.

"You know," Malcolm ran his tongue over his bottom lip with a light chuckle, "We were just talking about the planning of this wedding."

Senior's face lit up and excitedly started talking to Malcolm about the two of them getting married and starting a family. The whole idea of marrying Malcolm made her sick to her stomach. The sight of the two of them chomping it up like Malcolm wasn't living here on borrowed time, was sickening.

Taj's eyes narrowed at them before she mumbled to herself, "Should I leave so you two can enjoy the evening?"

Taj trailed off into her room and decided that Senior and Malcolm would be occupied with each other for at least another hour. Deciding to take a shower and wash her hair, she traveled into her bathroom. Staring at her reflection in the mirror, she analyzed the frown lines that settled into her face, the sadness that rested in her eyes, and the frown she developed.

"What happened to you Taj? Where did you go?" she whispered to herself. Dropping her head, she let the tears that she'd been holding back, fall from her eyes and glide down her cheeks. She quickly wiped her face and turned the shower on. As the steam immediately filled the shower, she climbed in and sat down on the wooden bench. The water saturated her hair, making it heavy and stretch down her back and beating over her bare skin massaging her tension away.

Again, she thought about Indie. That look in his eyes when he looked down at her, rested on her mind since she got back.

That look was full of every emotion but in that brief glance, Taj knew that he was missing the same thing she was. The light that drew them into one another in the first place.

With a deep inhale, Taj wiped the water from her face and started the process of washing her thick curly locks. Almost an hour later, she stepped out of the shower, wrapped up her hair and her body and walked back into the bedroom. She hadn't checked her messages in days, but she was curious; was he thinking about her as much as she was trying not to think about him?

She pulled her nightstand drawer open and pulled her new phone from the drawer. The door opened just as she was about to feed her temptation. "Your dad said he'll be back later to check on you."

Malcolm's voice filled the room and made Taj's face frown with her back turned to him. Lightly tapping the phone against her blue acrylic nails, she casually bit her lip and let the thoughts of Indie and anything he had going on, fade into the space around her.

As she was getting ready to turn around, Malcolm's hand tugged at the towel she had wrapped around her. Not missing a beat, Taj shrugged him off and stepped away from him. His brows pinned together with irritation. "We need to talk."

"That can happen without you touching me."

Taj's warning glare held strong until Malcolm groaned and took a step back. "We got to work this out Taj. I think that we need to start over. Let me make it right."

Taj rolled her eyes, absolutely sick and tired of the back and forth. "I think you need to give me my space. That's what I need. And that starts with you sleeping in the guest room."

Malcolm's jaw tightened and shot a look at her that he thought would make her falter on her statement. "Are you serious?"

"As a heart attack. I think it's cruel to kick you out with nowhere to go. So, let's just consider this as the beginning of starting over...apart."

His eyes flashed with anger again, but Taj knew that he wouldn't try anything with Senior in town. It didn't matter how pissed she was with her father; all it took was one phone call before Senior showed up ready to kick his ass for fucking with his daughter.

Malcolm turned around to walk to the door and stopped. "I'll go for a night but know that this isn't done. I'm not letting you go that easily."

Taj chuckled softly and said, "Yeah...okay. Whatever you say, Malcolm."

Escorting him out the door, she closed it and locked it behind him. Going back to the phone on her nightstand, she looked to see if Indie at least tried to reach out. There were texts for everyone but him. Taj rubbed her lips against each other before she grunted, locked her phone, and threw it back in the drawer. "Get yourself together, Taj."

Pulling the towel from her head, she walked back onto the bathroom to section, detangle and braid her hair in prep for tomorrow's day at the office. She had to get back to herself and Malcolm, nor Indie, was going to hold her back. Not anymore.

Chapter Eight

✤

I ndigo

AFTER THE OTHER DAY AT THE BANK, INDIE WAS LOOKING at Ricky sideways, but he couldn't do anything until Ricky showed him his hand. Until he did, Indie was going to move like everything was cool. Running his hand down his face, he groaned, "I need a fuckin' haircut."

Making a mental note to call Ajai later, Indie headed toward the buildings to see how the repairs were going. He knew he was about to walk into a headache, so he braced himself. Indie sunk into his seat and let his mind wander before pulling up on Ricky at the building complex.

Inhaling deeply, he looked over to his right and imagined Taj sitting in the passenger side with her feet propped up on the dash and singing along with the music. He typed out six different text messages and couldn't bring himself to send any of them. What he needed to say to her, needed to be said to her face so he could see it.

It was important to him that he fixed this, but he wasn't going to plant himself and force her to talk to him. That's not how he was going to fix this and get his girl back. If anything, it was bound to piss her off more than she already was. Truth be told, he was scared, and he could never bring himself to say it out loud.

The more he thought about Taj, he thought about being able to hold her and heal her broken pieces. Especially the pieces he was responsible for breaking. After that thought passed, faded images flashed in his head of the clown she was sharing her space with. Jealousy burned his flesh, thinking about Malcolm touching her and doing everything that he was supposed to be doing. It infuriated him the more he consumed himself with the thought. Feeling his face burn red, he shook his head and gritted his teeth. "This is so fucking stupid."

Pulling up to the complex, he parked his car behind Ricky's and climbed out. He walked down toward the end of the complex to find Leroy picking up some debris and putting it in a nearby trash can. "Indigo!" Leroy cheered, throwing his hand up toward Indie.

"What's going on nigga? You look good," Indie complimented, taking notice to Leroy's fresh white t-shirt and denim jeans. Feeling a smile creep over his face, Indie felt a sense of pride seeing that Leroy hadn't gone and drank his money away.

Indie and Leroy agreed that as long as he showed up to work on time every day and didn't drink, he would always have a job, food, and somewhere to lay his head. It seemed like Leroy had taken them seriously.

"Thanks, Indie. You look troubled," Leroy examined Indie before Indie reached out to shake his hand.

Indie frowned a bit and dropped his head. He couldn't get

Taj out of his head and lately the thought of her was more nagging than it had been in the last four years. He needed to get his family together, so everything he wanted had to sit on the back burner until time allowed him to get what he needed.

"I'm cool, man. No worries."

Leroy chuckled and shook his head. "Indigo...you got a lot on your shoulders. It looks heavy."

Indie looked up and glanced over his shoulder, with a slow nod of the head he looked back at Leroy. "Players fuck up some time you know?"

"But players get up too," Leroy spoke up before returning his attention back the debris on the floor. "They always get up."

Licking his dry lips, Indie pulled the door open to what was supposed to be the commercial office buildings. "Ay Ricky! What's going on?"

He walked down the hallway to find Ricky with his mouth balled up, looking at a few contracts. The tension could be cut with a knife. "Yo, what's goin' on?"

"These fuckers what another ten G's," Ricky informed, not taking his eyes off the contractors.

Indie drew his neck back and pushed his brows together. "For the fuck what?"

"The fucking ceiling is falling through," Ricky grunted. Indie turned his attention back to Ricky and chuckled. "Exactly. It's something new every day."

"Alright," Indie hummed. "Be real with me, how much is that going to cost to repair the roof. Ten grand ain't going to cut it, g."

The contractor growled lowly, realizing that he couldn't pull a fast one over Indie. Scratching the stubble of his beard, he hummed looking over his clipboard then at back up at Indie. "I can get it done for about six."

"That shit sounds a lot better," Indie nodded. "Go ahead and handle that for me."

Once the contractor left, Ricky looked at Indie with a scowl on his face. "Really? I've been arguing with that nigga for the last hour about the damn price. And he refused to come down."

"You know what it is?" Indie asked looking over at Ricky with a sly smirk on his face. "You don't have no fuckin' finesse. You just bark orders without building a rapport with anyone."

"Oh, word? Well handle this shit and I'll handle everything else."

"Uhh," Indie shook his head. "Teamwork nigga."

Just as Ricky was about to quip something back at him, Indie pulled his buzzing phone out of his pocket and looked down at the San Francisco number. "Hold up."

He answered the phone, "Hello."

"Hi, Indigo. It's Maria with BOLDnBLUE," Maria sounded off through the phone, almost like she was whispering into the phone. "How are you?"

"I'm cool," Indie answered slowly, looking over at Ricky. "Everything good?"

"It is, I'm not going to keep you long, I'm just calling to let you know that your grant has been approved. Congratulations." Indie could feel her smile through the phone, and it caused his lips to curl into one of its own. "When can you come for a meeting with Ms. Ali?"

He chuckled lightly and thanked God for assistance in the quest to get in a position to talk to Taj. "As soon as I need to."

"Alright, I will email you a few free days on her calendar and just let me know. We will handle your travel."

"There's no need for that. Just tell me when to show up."

"Alright, I'll be in touch. Have a good day."

"You too," Indie replied, before disconnecting their call.

Ricky waited for Indie to speak up and ask him what had him smiling so hard. "What you got going on?"

Indigo couldn't hide his smile. "I'm in there. The grant Joey put in with Taj's company got approved. Maria is going to set up a meeting."

"Don't blow it this time."

Indigo chuckled and pulled himself together. "Don't worry about it. I got it."

"You better because she's not answering me at all. You fucked it up for the rest of us."

"Yeah okay... listen, I got to meet up with Ajai so she can hook me up with a fade. Try not to fuck this up alright?"

Ricky grumbled something that Indie couldn't make out, so he turned his back and walked away. "Finesse, nigga!"

"Yeah, yeah, yeah."

Before Indie left, he slipped Leroy a few bills and headed toward Ajai to get his hair cut and talk to her about the news he had just received. He had an extra spring in his step and smile on his face that couldn't be wiped off by anything or anyone.

When he got to Ricky and Ajai's house, he reached in the glove box grabbed his gun and headed to the door. Locking his car, he opened the door and walked in the house. "Ajai, why is the door unlocked?"

He locked the door and walked further into the house.

"Bleu...I swear!" Ajai fussed from around the corner. Indie followed Bleu's fussing and Ajai's grunts into the guest bedroom they turned into Bleu's bedroom. Bleu was throwing a fight and Ajai looked like she was at her wit's end.

Stepping in to alleviate the situation, Indie handed Ajai the gun and scooped Bleu into his arms and tossed him into the air. "Why are you cryin', cuh? Huh? You ain't gotta cry, Uncle Indo is here and we're going to chill out. Cool out..."

Bleu hushed his crying and laid his head on Indigo's shoulder. Ajai huffed in relief, following the two of them out of the room. "He has been fighting sleep for hours and you get here, and he calms his ass down?"

Indigo chuckled lightly and stayed on the couch with Bleu resting peacefully in his arms. "First of all, I'm me. I got that touch."

"Yeah, whatever," Ajai groaned, putting the gun up. "If only you could keep that same energy when it comes to your girl."

Indie kissed his teeth, "Here we go."

"Yeah, here we go. It's like you just gave up on trying to get her back. We went through all that shit and because she's pissed, you fell back. That's some weak ass shit Indie."

"There's a child present," Indie tried to deflect Ajai, but she wasn't going to back down. With her hands on her hips, she looked up at him and knitted her brows together. "And if you must know, I got shit in the works."

"And what might that be? Because Taj is up there with the bum-ass nigga and she's about to marry him."

Indie kissed his teeth and rolled his eyes. "She ain't marrying that nigga."

"And she ain't marrying you," Ajai countered. "You keep dragging your feet and you're going to miss out. You thought four years was a long time, how does life sound."

Indie groaned and looked at her. "You know, right now I got to make sure the family shit is straightened out."

Ajai narrowed her eyes and curled her lip. "That's the damn problem, Indie. You are so concerned with saving everyone and cleaning up everyone else's mess that you have forgotten what it is to take care of yourself and take care of your needs. I don't care what you say or how you act, you need her. You won't be yourself until y'all are good. So, quit playing with me."

"I'm not playing with you," Indie assured, getting comfortable with Bleu in his arms.

Holding his nephew was causing him to relax and his eyes get heavy. With a yawn and a small stretch, he settled deeper into the couch and kicked his feet up on the coffee table. "If it were me, I would have had my ass there days ago and not letting up until she talked to me. Taj ain't the kind you just leave alone. She's smart and fine as hell and even if she breaks up with that weirdo, she probably has niggas at her door waiting on her. I'm telling you what I know Indie, do not miss your ship again."

Indie rolled his neck against the cushions of the couch and growled lowly to himself. "I came over here for a haircut but instead, I get another lecture. I'm worn out from all this Taj talk."

If he wasn't holding Bleu, he knew that Ajai probably would have smacked him upside the head for being stubborn but that was just the Leo in him.

"You are so fucking stubborn, it's annoying. When you can't have her, think about this conversation. I'm not bringing it up again. You are ridiculous."

Indie shut his eyes and thoughts of Taj really moving on past him, ignited that flame that he let fizzle out. He had to make sure that when he got to San Francisco, he applied all the pressure he could.

Untitled

Calm down, you know my heart can't take any more
Damn
Said this before
Do you remember you?
Do you remember who you were?
Do you remember you, do you remember who you were to me?
Jhene Aiko: Remember

Chapter Nine

jai

Snapping a picture of Indigo and Bleu passed out on the couch, Ajai sent it to Ricky with a text prompting him not to stay out all night. "They're so damn cute."

Leaning on the wall, she stared at the two of them a little longer before thinking about how Indie would be with his own children. With the woman made from him; Taj. Ajai dragged her eyes from Indie and Bleu, down to her phone. Unlocking her phone, she hovered her finger over Taj's name. Ajai went back and forth with herself chewing on the corner of her mouth. "Fuck it," she mumbled, hitting Taj's name and walking outside while it rang.

Tapping her nails against the table she waited until Taj answered. "Hello..."

Ajai's voice was caught in her throat. "Hello..." Taj's voice grew annoyed after the pause that she was experiencing. "Okay, I don't have time for this shit."

"Taj, it's me...Ajai." She pulled her bottom lip between her teeth and chewed on it, bracing herself for Taj's backlash.

"I wasn't expecting to hear from you," Taj sounded off with a soft huff that made Ajai tense up even more. "What's going on?"

Looking around her small backyard, she twirled her braids between her fingers. Unsure what to say, she looked back into the house at Indie and Bleu sprawled out across the couch completely comfortable and knocked out. "Honestly? I just wanted to check on you and see how you were doing...you know since everything went down."

Taj inhaled and then exhaled into the phone. "I'm good."

Instantly, Ajai knew that Taj was lying. Her words and her tone didn't match. She was anything but good and Ajai didn't know if it was her place to butt in and ask how she really was. "Are you really okay?"

Taj didn't answer. The silence that fell between them with their phones pressed to their ears, was uncomfortable. Ajai pulled the phone away from her ear and hit the FaceTime icon. She needed to look at her, listening to her try to coat her words weren't going to cut it.

Soon as Taj accepted the video call, Ajai lifted the phone to face level. "Now tell me, how you really are?"

"Ajai, does it really matter?" Taj's eyes looked away from the screen. Ajai studied her face and saw the unhappiness that she was trying her best to hide.

"Uh yes, it does. I really think you should have stayed here and worked everything out before you left."

Taj let out a hearty laugh that was full of sarcasm. "It is really getting old. Everyone has the same thing to say about how I handled everything. Honestly, that shit is fucked up. The whole situation is fucked up and the more time I take to dwell on it the longer I realize I'm not going anywhere."

Ajai frowned and studied Ajai's face through the screen. She knew if Indie waited any longer, Taj would be done and moving on. She didn't want that to happen, she knew just like they knew that they were meant to be.

"Do you miss him?" Ajai asked, knowing the answer was obvious but couldn't help but let it out and wait on Taj's answer. This time, she hoped the Taj gave her the truthful answer.

Taj sighed heavily and looked at Ajai. "Ajai, to say I don't would be a lie. You got to understand I looked for that man in everything for four years. I mourned, I went through depression, I even prayed the I could just feel him one more time. But to know that everything was a lie, makes me question if everything was real."

"Taj you need to talk to him."

"I'm not the one who hid for four years," Taj snapped. "It wasn't me. I lived that night over and over for four years."

"And so did he. He can't take it back; he can't change a damn thing. If you want to move on with him or just move on in general, you got to talk to him. Either you two are going to know who you are now...or close the chapter and move on without each other. But something has to happen and quickly. This weird space you two are in has everyone walking on eggshells at the mention of your name. He's pretending like he's okay and I know him. Indigo hasn't been okay in years."

Taj rested her chin on her knuckles and shrugged her shoulders. "I'm not the one who faked their death and I definitely won't be the one who reaches out to him. That's dead."

"I'm not saying that you have to, but when he calls just answer okay?"

"Alright, is that it?"

"Yeah, I just wanted to check on you and apologize how everything went down and see you."

"Thank you for calling me..." Taj spoke up after a couple of moments of silence. "I'm mad but it's not really at you."

"I know. You can't stay mad at me for too long," Ajai smiled. "Call me later?"

"I will."

Disconnecting their call, Ajai sighed and sat back in the chair and closed her eyes as the back door opened. She could smell Ricky's cologne and sweat hit her nostrils before he fully stepped out of the house. "You had a long day?"

"Long day is an understatement. I had a bunch of runs to make and then sit with the contractors all damn day," Ricky groaned, taking a seat by Ajai. "What you out here doing?"

"I just finished talking to Taj. She's still pissed. I can't say I blame her though. We all played a part in keeping this from her."

"Yeah, we did. As fucked up as it all might be. We chose our side to be on and unfortunately, it wasn't hers."

"Looking back on it we should have said something," Ajai huffed. "At least when everything died down."

"Yeah, but we can't take none of that shit back now. The ball is Indie's court to make that shit shake."

"You're right."

Ricky smirked and cut his eye at Ajai, "Say that again."

"No," she grunted before laughing. "Go take a shower."

"Only if you're coming with me. Looks like we got a babysitter."

"I'm with it," Ajai bit her bottom lip and popped up.

Ricky held her in her arms and kissed the top of her head, still riding the wave of their euphoria from the shower, to the bed. Ajai snuggled underneath him and threw her leg over him.

Ricky smirked softly and looked down at her. "I think you

need to go back to school and before you start the excuses, I've already talked to my mom and yours about keeping Bleu. You need some shit of your own."

Ajai peeled herself from under him and sat up. "Are you sure?"

"I am very sure."

Chapter Ten

T aj

"Hey," Maria greeted Taj as she stepped foot off of the elevator. Handing her a cup of tea, Maria smiled warmly hoping that tea, a doughnut, and smile would set Taj's mood for the day. Taj's scowl warned that it wouldn't do any good. "How was your night?"

Taj flashed Maria a frown and groaned after rolling her eyes. "Hmm Senior is here begging for forgiveness and wanting me to plan a wedding. Malcolm is sleeping in the guest room but keeps trying to find ways to come into the room and irritate the fuck out of me. So, it was a great night."

Maria frowned her face at the rundown of last night's events. If Taj were paying attention, she would notice that Maria's once cheery demeanor was now laced with the worry of how the next ten minutes would play out. "Uhh...we got to talk about your meetings today."

"Meetings? What meetings?" Taj stopped mid-stride and looked at Maria. "What is going on?"

"Nothing," Maria quickly replied, holding her breath and straightening her posture. "Nothing at all."

Taj's scowl intensified as she looked Maria up and down. "Are you going to tell me what is going on or am I going to find out by myself?"

"Uhh," Maria stammered, looking around the room for anything to break away from her glare and frown her lips. "Uhhh, just a potential investment..."

Taj pursed her lips and squinted her left eye and raised her right brow. "Spit it out, please. Tea and a doughnut, you are really laying it on thick, aren't you? But for what? Why is my door closed?"

"You have a grant recipient in your office and..." Maria paused, seeing Taj raise her brow even higher and put the cup of tea down along with the doughnut.

"Hand me the file, please." Taj held her hand out for the file tucked underneath Maria's arm. Maria shook her head, knowing that Taj was just a few minutes from hitting the roof and storming out of here. "Maria, the file."

Reluctantly Maria handed the file over and chewed nervously on her lip. Taj dragged her eyes from Maria to the papers in the file. "Grant approved for the technology center in Los Angeles ordered to Indigo Si –"

Taj's eyes fluttered quickly, and her mouth ran dry. She closed it and tried to pull herself back together after becoming completely undone inside. "Is he in there?"

"He's been waiting on you since I got here this morning," Maria admitted. "Taj, please don't be mad at me. I saw the request come across my desk and had to jump at it. It's been too long and you two have to talk."

Taj balled her mouth up and shook her head in disbelief. There was no way Indie flew up here to get a grant. He wanted more than just funding; Taj knew exactly what he wanted because she wanted it too but giving in to him too easily would mean that he possibly wouldn't respect the fact that her feelings in this mattered. She needed him to understand the extent of the damage he'd done and the only way she could make that be known was to turn him away.

"He's in my office?" Taj asked again just so she could finish her process.

Maria nodded her head before Taj took off to the bathroom down the hall to do a quick adjustment to her Ralph Lauren button-up and skinny blue jeans. Applying another coat of gloss to her lips and fluffing her curls, she huffed and walked out of the bathroom like she had all her emotions together. It was anything but; she was a mess.

"Pull it together, T. You've turned people down before...just don't look in his eyes." Taj coached herself as she marched back down the hall with her chest poked out and her head held high.

She was still angry but what her heart wanted and what her brain said were two different things. Taj wanted to run into her office and wrap her arms around Indie and just inhale his scent. Feel his arms around her and his heartbeat against her eardrum. Her brain was fighting for her to take back the control and send him stepping.

Taj slowed her march down to a slow stroll down the hall with her head still held high. She was a professional and this was her place of business. She wasn't going to let Indie's presence cause her to get upset and act out of character. Not for a second time, anyway. Grabbing her tea and her doughnut, she walked past Maria and into her office.

Opening the door to her office, she caught Indie staring at her awards displayed around the walls. It was almost like he was lost in a trance of her accomplishments without him. There was a slight smirk of pride on his face as he traced his fingers over her degree. Taj could tell he was consumed in his own thoughts, but he could have those somewhere else. Clearing her throat, she walked further into the office. "Mr. Sims."

He turned around and studied her. She could feel his eyes on her and the motions that she was trying to let go of came rushing in. Even anger, that was the most powerful of them all. She cut her eyes at him and dropped her bags down. She shut the door and looked him and down like he owed her money. Then she pressed her back against it, folded her arms, and looked up at him step away from the wall and take a step closer.

"Why the hell are you here?" she groaned with a roll of the eyes when he connected eyes with hers. She had to stay angry with him because if she didn't, she would be begging to feel him. The energy in the room intensified more by the second, making her chest tighten.

Indie placed his hand in his pockets and swayed in the spot he was standing in. He simply droned, "My investment."

"Tuh," she grunted, scratching the back of her neck and walking past him to her chair. "Yeah, that's up in the air since once again, everyone worked around me."

"Taj let me just..." Indie started up only for Taj to cut him off.

"Leave. I can let you just leave, so please go," she forced, knowing damn well she wanted him to stay.

Indie shot her a look, trying his best not to get aggravated with her stubbornness. "What?"

"Did I stutter!" Taj snapped, looking up at him with tears

threatening to spill over. She attempted to yell again but her voice came out in a whisper. "Leave, Indigo. Just get out."

Indie shook his head no and advanced toward her desk before she held her hands up. "Give me a damn minute. All I need is a minute of your time."

Taj's head whipped in a circle, watching him step closer to her. The closer he got to her the more her stomach knotted up and her mouth ran dry. He smelled amazing, looked ever better, and his eyes danced with fire. That was a clear indication that she needed him to get away from her before she became putty in his hands. "Another one? You've taken up minutes, hours, days, months, and years of my damn life! What the fuck else do you want from me? Hm? I've given you all I have and quite frankly, I'm fucking tired and over it."

Indie clenched his jaw and looked at her face twisted and contoured with pain and anger. Taj stared into his and saw the reflection of her feelings and a heavy amount of regret knitted his emotions together. "Baby, I'm sorry."

He reached out for her and she backed up. There wasn't too much space for her to go but into the wall and if she got trapped, this would be the end of the fight.

"Don't," she snapped. "Don't you dare call me Baby. You lost the fucking right. And sorry isn't going to give me back my fucking time!"

Indie pinched the bridge of his nose and clenched his jaw in frustration. He wanted what she wanted but the electric fence she just put between them was making it more difficult than he thought it would be. "You got to know that, I'm sorry. I didn't mean to break your heart or waste your time. Shit just got crazy and I couldn't—"

She folded her hands across her chest and curled her lips. Taj was starting to shut down, that was the only option she had left. She refused to break down and cry in front of him, not again. His apology was now falling on reluctant ears. She cut him a nasty look and looked up at him up and down.

"Aight," he gritted his jaw and took a bigger step toward backing her into the wall. It was a power play to take back control of the situation. "You got it. This is your place of business. I only need the investment to get this tech center up and going and I'll be out your way."

She grunted, looking him up and down again. Dropping her arms, she pushed him back with a grunt. Indie attempted to grab her arms as he stepped backward. Taj snarled, "A suit that didn't come from the sale rack, polished wingtip shoes and a crisp white shirt underneath your navy-blue designer suit. No."

"What did you say?" he questioned, looking at Taj with a grim expression.

"You heard me. The answer is no, I'm not investing in anything you have going on. Not as long as you're in the streets."

Indie fixed his mouth to reply but she threw her hand up. "Aht, aht. Fool me once shame on you, fool me twice...I will not be fooled again. I will not have my clean money tied up in any of your shit. The answer is no, Mr. Sims."

"Cut the Mr. Sims shit out, Baby," he grumbled.

"Yet again, Mr. Sims, I've asked you to leave."

Indie clenched his jaw and frowned in agitation. She was being a lot more difficult than she had to be, but Indie needed to understand that he couldn't fuck her over twice. Once was more than enough for her and she was still living with the stench of that betrayal.

"Baby," Indie said her name in a warning tone as though it could sway her.

"I just told you not to call me that. The decision is final."

Rubbing his thumb over his bottom lip, he nodded his head. "I won't stop coming here until I get what I want, Baby."

She snorted in laughter and shook her head. "You can show up a million times a month but you're not getting the investment."

Indie watched her intently as she sat down in her seat and kicked her feet up on the desk. "You know damn well that it's not the investment I want."

"Oh yeah?" she dryly questioned. "Then what is it?"

"You," he replied, watching as her breath got caught in her throat. "So, Baby, I'll be seeing you soon. Eventually, you'll break down and talk to me. Next time keep the dramatics to a two."

Taj snorted once more, "Don't hold your breath."

Waiting for him to walk out of her office, she dropped her head back the minute the door closed behind him. Closing her eyes, she inhaled and exhaled in attempts to get her emotions to level out and her feet not want to run behind him. After all these years, he still had a hold on her. Indie could tell her the sky was purple and she would believe him. Her heart still belonged to him, there wasn't a question about that but there was damage done and it was going to take more than one investment and pop-up to fix her heart.

Chapter Eleven

❧

I ndigo

INDIE BARRELED THROUGH THE PARKING GARAGE OF THE office building where Taj's company was located and attempted to keep his cool until he got in his car. As soon as he climbed inside his car, he let out a loud roar of frustration. Not because things didn't go his way but because Taj was playing a game. The game of How Tough Can You Be, was bound to go left quickly if she didn't stop soon.

He ran his hand down his face and reset himself. He came here with the intention of leaving with Taj in his good graces and he wasn't going to leave until he got his way. He didn't care if he had to show up every day and wait outside the building; he was going to do it until they put everything on the table and came to an understanding. And the only understanding he was going to accept, was her hand in his. Nothing else would suffice but that.

Starting the engine, Indie pulled out the garage and headed to the hotel. Indie got halfway to the hotel and decided to divert and grab something to eat. After dinner and a couple of drinks, he made his way to the hotel to settle in for the night. When he got inside the room, he pulled off his suit jacket and called Ricky. He plopped down on the couch and looked around the room. If Taj took the time to hear him out, she would have known that even though Joey requested the grant, he didn't need it. The street money he made was more than enough to float the tech center. And once the other businesses were up and running, he wouldn't need to be in the streets anymore.

"What's going on?" Ricky asked upon answering the call.

Indie let out a huff and closed his eyes. "I pride myself on staying in control and not coming out of pocket, but I almost shook the shit out of her. When did she get so fuckin' stubborn?"

Ricky's laugh was so loud that Indie had to pull the phone away from his ear. "When? She's been stubborn, you were just smitten and didn't see it."

"Turn your volume down, please."

"Don't get snappy with me, nigga. Put your best foot forward and get your woman. She's going to fight you until the end because that's just how she is now. You think if she didn't have to fight for so long, she would be doing it now by choice?" Ricky planted the seed for Indie's wheels to turn.

"Nigga, what you just say?" Indie pinned his brows together, like Ricky was standing in front of him.

Ricky scoffed softly. "What did you think I just said...you slow?"

"Don't fuck with me," Indie grunted. "I wish that nigga would look at her crazy."

Ricky laughed again and sighed. "You weren't there to see how the bitch ass nigga was running around like he lost his fuckin' mind when she took her ring off. I can assure you he's lookin' and talkin' crazy. How you handlin' that?"

"Don't worry about that. How's everything going down there? How much more product do we have to move?"

Ricky's pause in answering the question only added more irritation to Indie's suspicion. He only asked to see if Ricky was going to tell him the truth. Until then, he was willing to sit back and watch how Ricky maneuvered around when he thought that he wasn't looking. Ricky would end up exposing his hand sooner than later and when he did, Indie would address it. Until then, he shifted his priorities from the streets and making sure everyone was doing what they were supposed to do, to getting Taj back and making sure all his legal businesses could create a nest egg.

"You deaf nigga?" Indie barked through the phone.

"Calm yo ass down nigga," Ricky returned. "We'll be out in about a month if they keep moving work like this."

"How much is it going to be after everyone gets their cut?"

"About 200," Ricky informed.

"Alright bet, I'll be back in a couple of days," Indie announced, giving Ricky just enough rope to let him run free. "I need to see how much I can wear her down."

"May the force be with you," Ricky chuckled before they disconnected.

Indie inhaled and pushed himself off the couch and walked over to the window and looked out at the bay. Ricky had done a great job of riling Indie up about how Taj's life was with Malcolm. Thinking about how Taj reacted when he towered over her, he clenched his jaw and tense up himself. She was too comfortable with him approaching her like that. Even though he wasn't overly aggressive, he didn't like how she was okay with that.

Closing his eyes, he washed the thought of Malcolm and thought about her. This time he got a better look at her. She filled out. Her hips were wider, her breasts were fuller and even her ass got fatter. As beautiful as she was and as much as her body made him brick up that imposter still lingered in the background. The reality of the situation that Taj was promised to another man. His woman, the one who he gave his heart to, the one whose touch could set him on fire and cooled him off at the same time, was months away from being gone.

"Fuck," Indie grunted, running his hand over his head. "What the fuck are you going to do?... What the fuck am I going to do?"

Dropping his head, he walked back over to his phone, he pulled her name up on the screen. Tapping her name, he pressed the number and put the phone on speakerphone, hoping that she would answer.

Just as the phone was getting ready to send him to voice-mail, it was picked up and the voice on the other end was anything but welcoming. "Who the fuck is this?"

Indie instantly glowed red and the liquor in his system wasn't helping his tongue from lashing out. "Look cuh, I ain't that nigga you wanna fuck with. Where is Taj?"

"She's busy," Malcolm replied. "Fuck you calling her for?"

"Muthafucka, I want to. That's why. Listen, I ain't doing this shit with you. I know how to get in touch with her. Don't worry."

"Is that a threat?" Malcolm bucked through the phone like it was going to shake Indie up.

Indie chuckled and licked his lips. "Nah, it's a fuckin' promise. I'll be seeing you, though."

Hanging up the phone, Indie's flame was roaring and he was going to stop at nothing until Taj was his again.

Chapter Twelve

※※

T aj

WALKING INTO HER HOUSE THE LAST PERSON SHE WANTED
to see was Malcolm and Senior, chomping it up in the kitchen.
Snarling at both of them, she tossed her phone on the counter
and then dropped her purse down. "Why are you here?"

"I was hoping you would take me back to the airport?"

"Did I pick you up from the airport?" she countered,
cutting Senior a look.

Malcolm scoffed and shook his head. "Don't talk to him like
that."

Scoffing softly, Taj looked Malcolm up and down, "Don't
talk to me."

"Taj, what the hell is wrong with you?" Senior questioned
not happy by her attitude.

Taj looked at the two and grunted, "Looking at you two is really nailing the coffin shut on a bad day. Matter of fact, come on. The faster I get you to the airport, the faster I can get over my attitude."

Picking her purse back up and leaving her phone on the counter, she turned to the door. She purposely left her phone behind so she wouldn't have to be bothered by the texts that Indie sent earlier. Walking out of the house and down the hall, to the elevator, she crossed her arms over her body and waited for it to arrive at her floor. Senior's breathing was heavy and traveled down the hall behind her.

She didn't say a word to him until they were five minutes away from the airport. The only reason she spoke up was because Senior said, "I'm not trying to have our relationship like this, Taj."

"You don't think you should have thought about that before you lied to me?"

Senior huffed and shook his head. "Baby, you're being dramatic."

"Oh, I haven't even begun to be dramatic, Charles. Just imagine mom went into hiding and everyone knew she was alive but you. How would you feel? Fucking pissed and disgusted."

"Watch your mouth, Taj Ali Adams," Senior spoke up with a stern voice. "I am your father, give me that respect."

"And I am your grown-ass daughter that you had mourning and depressed for no damn reason. Where was the respect for me? Oh, I forgot that was protection. You might be my father, but you are very unfamiliar to me. I don't do well with unfamiliar people in my presence."

Senior gripped his temples and groaned with aggravation coursing through his veins. "You are just as stubborn as your mother. I'm not trying to fight with you. Honestly, I'm tired of fighting with you. We are all we have left."

Taj nodded her head slowly as she pulled into the airport drop off point. "We are, and I've been present without any secrets and all the respect I could muster up for you. You... haven't been and that will forever be my issue until I'm ready to forgive you. Today ain't the day. Doesn't mean that I don't love you, but I need my time away from all of it to sort through my feelings. Quite honestly, you and Malcolm are at the top of my shit list."

Senior looked at Taj and raised his brow. "What's going on with you and Malcolm?"

"This farce of an engagement is soon to end," Taj admitted. "Don't try to talk me out of it. I can't take too much more of this shit."

"Taj," Senior huffed. "That man loves you."

She scoffed and unlocked the door. "Yeah, Indie loved me too. I felt how that ended. Not doing it again. Have a safe flight."

Senior got out of the car and looked down at his daughter. "I love you, daughter, and everything I do will forever be in your best interest. Don't throw the towel in on Malcolm yet."

With an eye roll, Taj nodded her head before pulling off from the curb once he closed the door. She could yell and scream about how Senior protected Malcolm's baby feelings more than hers, but she was sick of beating a dead horse. She got herself in this situation and she was going to get out somehow, someway. Although Malcolm had proven himself to be her constant comfortable spot in all its uncomfortableness, she couldn't stay in that spot anymore.

"Ugh," she groaned, peeling her heels from her feet as she walked into the house. Massaging them lightly, she looked up to see Malcolm slamming her phone down on the counter with a twisted expression. "Dare I ask what the fuck is wrong with you?"

"Indie just called you... fuck is going on?" Malcolm questioned, making Taj knit her brows.

"You really got to get some business that ain't mine," she huffed, walking over the counter and grabbing her phone.

"Why is he calling you?"

"Do I look like I know? You're the one who answered the got damn call. You need to calm the fuck down."

Malcolm towered over her and clenched his jaw. The look in his eyes was threatening enough. Every encounter they had was becoming more intense than the previous. "Taj, it would be smart not to test my limits anymore."

She scoffed and turned away, only provoking him to grab her by the arm and yank her back. She tried to hold her composure, but she was afraid. "Get your hands off me."

"Don't fuck around and lose the best thing you have going, for that nigga who left you hanging." Malcolm's glare got stronger along with his grip, making Taj wince slightly. "Stop being stupid, Taj. I've already told you once, I wasn't letting you go. Don't make me have to show what I mean."

Letting her go, Malcolm stomped off to the guest room leaving Taj with tears cradled in the ducts of her eyes. Instead of letting them fall, she inhaled deeply and held it before releasing. Wincing as she touched her arm, gathered her belongings off the counter and headed to her room. Locking the door behind her, she pulled off her shirt and took notice of the bright red mark Malcolm left behind.

"This nigga has really lost his mind," she grumbled, picking her phone up off the dresser and scrolling to see a few texts from Indie.

I'm not leaving until we talk.

This has gone for long enough...

You took my heart and I don't want it back...I just want you

Taj hummed and rolled her lips over one another and fell back on the bed. "This is too much."

Untitled

You don't be on that bullshit
You gon' hold me down always
That's why I'm fucking with you
All I want is you
You so amazing.
Eric Bellinger: That's Why

Chapter Thirteen

R icky

"Ay Rick!" Manny shouted as Ricky pulled up to his mother's house. Glancing over his shoulder, he saw Manny walking across the street toward him. Shutting the door of the car, Ricky traveled to the trunk and perched himself up.

"What up, nigga? What you need?"

"Ain't shit," Manny replied, stopping at the edge of the driveway. "We are about out of this shit."

Ricky hadn't filled everyone with his plan and letting Manny in on it, possibly meant it getting back to Indie and causing more of a rift between them. Ricky knew that once Indie's trust was broken it was hell getting back in his good graces. Ricky saw Indie handle niggas for less and tensed up at the possibility of Indie getting wind of this.

Sliding off the trunk of the car, Ricky looked up and down

the block then back at Manny and pulled the rest of the product out his pocket and handing it over to him. "You get rid of that tonight and hit me up, I'll have more for you."

"I thought we were –"

Ricky cut him off. "What I just say?"

Manny nodded slow, stuffing the baggies in his pocket. "I got you."

"Aight, bet. Get out of here before twelve starts sniffin' around me."

Manny pulled himself away and started back up at the street. Ricky surveyed the block one more time and strolled into his mother's house.

"Ma!" he called out the small home, expecting to see her sitting on the couch watching the tv. "Where you at?"

Mary pulled her bedroom door closed and hurried down the hall to pop her son upside the head. "Ow ma. You're going to stop hitting me across the head like that."

"Because you walk in my house loud as hell like you don't have no got damn sense. I just put your son down for a nap," Mary fussed, walking away from her son. "Why are you here? I thought you had things to do?"

"Where is Ajai?" Ricky asked, frowning his face at her response.

Mary shrugged. "Something about enrolling in school. Why am I looking at you?"

"Damn ma, I can't come see how you're doing?" Ricky curled his lip up and sat down at the table. "You acting like you got more than my son up in here."

"Son," Mary scoffed. "If I had a man in here, I would have changed the locks."

Ricky's lip curled more. "Don't play with me like that, ma."

"I ain't playing. Considering I haven't seen you since we dropped that bomb on your cousin, I'm surprised to see you."

"I've been busy," Ricky defended.

Mary scoffed again and nodded her head slowly. "Does any of this busy business include you making Ajai an honest woman?"

Ricky rose his brow and looked at his mother like she was speaking out the side of her neck. "Lady you smoking crack?"

Mary spun around to smack his head again. "You got to be getting high off your own supply talking to me crazy. You heard me the first time."

"Ma," Ricky chuckled and shook his head. "Where is all this coming from? Ajai and I are cool. We good where we at."

"You think y'all good where y'all at, like you got tomorrow or the next day or the next? You of all people should know it's not promised. So at least give her what she deserves, Ricky."

Ricky dropped his body back in the set and scratched the nape of his neck with a twisted expression his face. "You trying to give a nigga anxiety with that 'M' word and shit?"

"First of all, you been stuck on them sorry ass Lakers for years and you can't commit to the woman who rode for you through everything and bore you a son. She doesn't complain about anything and you're just going to dismiss that because you're scared. Real niggas put their family first."

Ricky drew his neck back and placed his hand on his chest like he was offended by Mary talking to him in the only way he was going to understand. "Ma, your mouth."

"Oh, you understood that huh? Get your shit together and be a man about his family. All the fast money and shit will fade. If Ajai is what you want, you'll rise to the occasion and not just when it comes to making a baby."

"On that note, I'm about to go." Ricky sighed and pushed himself up from the table before giving his mother one last glance over his shoulder. Only to see Mary with pursed lips and her arms folded of her chest. "I'll see you later. I got a few more moves to make."

"Mmhmm. Be safe out there boy."

"Be safe in here," Ricky called before walking out the door and headed down the steps to his car.

Cruising down the street with the windows down to welcome the breeze, the words that his mother let out into the atmosphere played in his mind. There wasn't a secret that he loved Ajai. She was the better part of him, and she deserved everything she wanted. Ricky's fear was holding him, hostage, he could leave them at any moment.

His attention was pulled from his thoughts to a car speeding down the street with a few guys hanging out the window, firing shots down the streets. Ricky ducked and swerved his car over the curb, hitting the light pole causing the airbags to deploy just as a few stray bullets pierced the side of his car and hitting him in the arm.

"Ah fuck!" he shrieked, grabbing his arm. The smell of the tires burning down the street indicated that the drive-by was over but the sound of screams and gunshots were replaced with sirens and people pouring into the streets to assist.

It took three people to pull Rick from the car, including two cops. For a brief moment, he was happy he unloaded all his product off on Manny but that was quickly replaced by having to take a ride to the hospital.

He was sure not to say anything to Ajai or Indie, until the bullet was removed from his arm. The drugs dripping through his IV helped him relax. He was so tense that he hadn't taken in what just happened. No one was trying to kill him but if he hadn't ducked, they would have. His life could have been over and Ajai and Bleu would be here without him. He needed to make a move.

Grabbing his phone with the mobile hand, he shot Manny a

quick text telling him to handle the shipment later. He hated that he had to pull Manny into his shit but it was necessary, the last thing he wanted to do was piss off any connections. Hitting Ajai's name, he pressed the phone to his ear and waited on her to pick up.

"Hey babe," she answered. Ricky could hear the happiness in her voice and hated to ruin it. "What's up?"

"Leave Bleu with Ma and come down to the hospital," he rumbled.

"Why what's wrong?" her tone went from happy to distraught. "Ricky, what happened?"

"Ain't shit really. I just got shot."

Chapter Fourteen

 jai

"GOD, I KNOW WE DON'T TALK OFTEN BUT PLEASE LET HIM be okay," Ajai whispered to herself as though someone else was in the car listening to her desperate plea for mercy. "I cannot lose him yet." She was used to losing people she cared about but losing Ricky would be like losing herself. He would take her soul with him, if he were to leave her and Bleu alone. The gas pedal was pressed to the floorboard as she sped to the hospital.

Parking the car and killing the engine, she ran into the building and frantically searched for his room. Unsure of what she was about to walk into, she pulled out her phone and called Indie. The phoned trilled in her ear as she gnawed at the corner of her mouth, anxiously ready to get on the elevator and lay her eyes on Ricky.

In a whirlwind, she almost ran into the receptionist desk. "What room is Ricky Adams in?"

The nurse behind the desk, dragged her eyes from her computer to Ajai. Normally, Ajai was composed, the nurse's slothfulness was going to cause the other side of her to rear its ugly head. "Who?"

Ajai growled lowly to herself and squinted her eyes at the nurse. "Ricky...Adams...what room is he in?"

"Yo, what's up sis?" Indie asked lazily.

The nurse dragged her eyes from Ajai and rolled them heavily. "He's in room 406."

Taking off around the counter, she bolted to the elevator. "Ricky's been shot! He didn't tell me anything just that he was shot. I don't know what I'm walking into. He called me like everything was cool," Ajai informed him while repeatedly pressing the button for the floor. If it took the doors any longer to close, she was going to take off to the stairs.

"What the hell you just say?" Ajai could hear the spring in Indie's voice. "What the fuck happened? Who did it? I'm on my way."

"I don't know, I'm about to walk into his room right now," Ajai replied as the elevator dinged and the doors were pulled open, allowing her to rush down the hall and slowly push Ricky's door open.

The sight of Ricky propped up in the hospital bed high from the meds and sipping a juice box while the nurse dressed his arm, sent fire through Ajai. "Indie. Stay where you are, this nigga is fine."

"You sure?" Indie questioned.

Ajai growled, "Oh I'm sure."

Still gripping the phone, she narrowed her eyes at Ricky and made her way over to the other side of the bed. "You're sitting in here drinking a juice box and I'm thinking you're about to die. What kind of shit is this?"

"Good shit," he smirked. "I can't feel a got damn thing. I'm floating."

The nurse giggled, causing Ajai to cut her eyes at her and look her up and down. "He ain't that damn funny."

"I'm not? You've been lying to me this whole time?" Ricky questioned, looking up at Ajai who still had the phone pressed to her ear. Without looking at the nurse, Ricky warned. "My girl likes to fight...don't get rocked to sleep like a baby."

"This nigga," Indie huffed in her ear. "Ay, sis, when he's off the shit I'll call to figure everything out. Keep me posted aight?"

"I will," Ajai assured him before hanging up and punching Ricky in his good arm. "I should shoot you my damn self for getting me all worked up like this. I ran a million red lights; I was swerving in and out of lanes so I could get here to check on you."

"Please don't make those sorts of threats in front of me," the nurse spoke up, bringing the attention back to her.

Ricky whistled and chuckled. He may have been high off the meds, but he knew that Ajai had slapped women for less, just for looking in his direction. "Girl, you better stop talkin'."

Ajai cut her eye over to the nurse and picked her apart without saying a word. She was pretty, and ample in all the right places. That wasn't a threat; Ajai was secure in who she was and Ricky hadn't strayed in all the years they'd been together. What was pissing her off was this nurse's inability to stay the fuck out of their conversation. Ajai needed her to do her job and not try to get extra attention from Ricky.

"Bitch, do you mind shutting the fuck up and let me talk to my man? You've over there giggling and keke-ing and shit. You want something to ke-ke about? How does an ass-whooping sound? Hmm? Not keke-ing now are you? I'll knock your fuckin' lights out if you try me again."

The nurse's face lost color and her eyes grew wide. "Uh...I was just laughing."

"Uh...uh.. you were just asking for me to kick your ass and dog walk you. Say something else," Ajai warned, prepared to hold up her end of the bargain.

The nurse said nothing.

"That's what the fuck I thought," Ajai motioned for her to finish what she was assigned to do, with a twirl of her finger in the direction of the sling she was trying to put on. Adjusting the last strap on Ricky's sling, the nurse quickly made herself scarce. Ajai smacked her lips as the nurse walked out. "Don't let these hoes hype you up. I already told you about that. I was about to slap her teeth out her got damn head."

Ricky laughed softly and put his juice box down. Ajai could look in his eyes and tell that pretty soon he was going to be knocked out. "You know, I'm not trying to hype nobody up but you. It's cute that you're still jealous over a young nigga."

"Yeah whatever, young nigga." Ajai rolled her eyes heavily and waved his comment off. "How did this happen?"

She couldn't stay upset with him long, plus he looked so pitiful propped up in the bed, seeing purple elephants and chuckling to himself at whatever was going on in his head. Adjusting his blanket over him, she hummed softly and placed her hand on top of his.

"Hood niggas," Ricky shrugged. "Having a shootout in broad day, stray bullets were flying. I yanked the steering wheel, crashed the car into the light pole, and got shot."

Hearing that made her tense up. It was a part of the life they lived but she was tired of living like this. Looking over her shoulder and hoping that no one ever delivered bad news about him, to her. "You say it like it's nothing. Like it's not a big deal that you got shot."

Ricky shook his head no and sighed. "It is something. Before all that shit broke out, I was thinking about Bleu and you...what would happen if I lost y'all or if y'all lost me. I don't want to live that reality and I damn sure don't want you to live with it. We got to get the fuck out the hood."

Ajai couldn't help but agree; Ricky was completely right. He wrapped his hand around hers and brought her knuckles to his lips. "I love you. I don't say it often because words will always fail but don't anybody got me like you got me. You've proved that time and time and time again."

Shrugging her shoulders, she looked down at him as he settled into the bed and closed his eyes. "It's nothing baby. That's what I'm supposed to do, Bonnie and Clyde."

"How about Mr. and Mrs.?"

Ajai's eyes shot out of her head and watched as Ricky's breathing became relaxed. "What did you say?"

"You heard me. Marry me, let's make this shit official," he droned.

Ajai wasn't sure if it was the drugs talking or Ricky, so she was choosing to be very careful with her response. Getting ready to open her mouth and tell Ricky to go to sleep, he started singing.

"Baby, I'm at the point in my life and I'm tired of playing games. I'm ready to settle down, I'm ready to buy a house and I'm ready to change my last name...your last name...I'm ready to have more kids. I'm ready for the life to live, and all the love to give...you've been my Superwoman for so long, I'm ready for you to be my wife," Ricky's altered version of *4Ever* by Lil' Mo made Ajai burst out in a fit of giggles.

"Ricky, go to sleep," she giggled, lightly slapping his chest and sitting in the seat by him. "I'm not doing this with you today."

"I want you to do it to me and with me every day," he tiredly responded.

When Ajai glanced up at him, he'd dozed off. Grabbing the extra blanket at the end of the bed, she followed suit. The chair wasn't comfortable, but it was the first time in two years that she wasn't sleeping with Bleu attached to her. Curling up in the chair, she got as comfortable and she could and drifted off.

After a few hours of sleeping, she cracked her eyes open to see another nurse, who was less attractive and feigning for less attention than the first one, redressing Ricky's wound. The meds were now worn off and he winced slightly in pain at the cold air of the hospital room, hitting the open wound.

"That shit hurts like a bitch," he spoke up with gritted teeth.

Ajai fully woke up and stretched. She sat back and watched the nurse dress the wound, clean up and leave. "How are you feeling?"

"Waiting for this damn drip to kick in. That bitch went right through my arm."

Ajai winced for him and shook her head. "I would have died."

"I know you would have, that's why I be on your ass about moving around by yourself. You give any thought about what I asked you earlier?"

Ajai's brow popped up and a snort escaped her lips. "You were serious? I thought you were just playing around."

"Playing? I put on my good singing voice for you." Ricky scoffed like he was offended. "I'm not bullshitin' when it comes to you and our son. I am one hundred about locking you down for real."

"And me locking you down too." Ajai let a small smile crept across her face. "You sure you ready for this?"

"What's going to be different? We already got everything but the title," Ricky informed her. "I don't have a ring or anything right now, but I got you."

"You're serious, huh?" Ajai asked again, just to be sure.

"As a got damn heart attack. You're my girl. I love you," Ricky droned, making Ajai smile wide and show all her pretty teeth.

"Well, if you say it like that...yes I'll marry you." Ajai scooted over to the side of the bed and kissed his lips. "But I want my ring."

"I got you. The ring, the house, the salon. Whatever you want, baby you got it," Ricky assured. "Whatever you want."

"All I want is you out of here and home with Bleu and me. This chair is uncomfortable," Ajai huffed.

"Trust me, all I want is to be home with y'all too. Indie ain't on his way here is he?"

"Nah just me and you. But he said he was going to call later and check-in." Ajai rubbed her hand over Ricky's low cut. "Just want to you get home and we can think about everything else. Okay?"

Ricky kissed the knuckles of her hand and settled back into the hospital bed, "Get up here and lay by me. Don't tell me no either."

"Ricky, I'm not fuckin' you in here," Ajai warned.

He smacked his lips and chuckled. "Can a nigga just cuddle? Damn."

"You don't ever want to cuddle boy, I know better than that."

"You're about to know something else, too."

83

Chapter Fifteen

Indie

WITH HIS HAND CLASPED BEHIND HIS HEAD, INDIE STARED at the ceiling consumed with thoughts of Taj, the streets, and the business. These were the normal morning thoughts on a loop. But this morning, he was wanting to feel her warmth, reach over and placed his hand on the curve of her neck. What Indie tried to push off to the back of his mind was now in the forefront and stubbornly rooted itself into his brain until he acknowledged his. There wasn't anything about her that he didn't miss. From the cut of her beautiful brown eyes down to the gnashing of her teeth.

He rolled over to his side and grabbed the phone off the charger. Studying the screen, he had a few notifications from Ajai, saying that Ricky was going home and a few from his mom.

Nothing from Taj. He was hopeful. Malcolm could bark and gnash his teeth like a rabid dog all he wanted but he was going to learn that there was a bigger and badder dog that wasn't backing down. He really didn't see Malcolm as a threat, and he would never flinch at his threats and demands. However, he was going to enjoy fucking with him in the process of taking Taj back.

As Indie scrolled through his text messages the phone started to buzz, swiping the screen, he answered. "Hello."

"You have a collect call from an inmate at the Los Angeles Inmate Reception Center, do you accept?"

"Yeah." Indie swung his legs over the bed and sat up. He leaned forward and rested his elbows on his knees and waited for Joey's voice to flow through the phone.

"What's up, Indie?" Joey asked cheerfully. That made Indie smile, cheerfulness meant that Joey was holding his ground and keeping his head up. "How's everything?"

"You sound good, cuh," Indie smirked softly. "Everything good, ain't nobody trying you?"

Joey chuckled. "Nah ain't nobody trying me, cuh. It's cool. Bobby came through yesterday."

"Oh bet? What is he talking about?" Indie asked with a yawn.

"There's a break in the case, he's looking at me getting out on a lesser charge and a couple of months of probation. Bobby said he'll contact you soon," Joey informed. "I'm ready to get out this shit."

"I know you are; I'll talk to Bobby and find out what needs to happen," Indie muttered, standing to his feet and stretching. He couldn't help but smile, a break in the case meant that Joey would be home sooner than later as long the county didn't try to pull no funny shit and keep him longer. Indie felt for Joey, although this was the direct consequence of Joey disobeying

85

orders, Indie still didn't wish being locked up on anyone and he was hell-bent about not going back.

"Talk to me, tell how everything is going with Taj?" Joey asked making Indie huff a little, replaying back the encounter with her. "That huff tells me not according to plan."

"I already told you that we're not spending your call talking about me," Indie replied, walking toward the window of the hotel. "Your books good?"

"Indie," Joey gave him a huff of his own and what Indie imagined to be a heavy eye roll. "Nigga. I don't call to talk about me. I'm locked up, that's that. What's going on with my baby?"

Indie chuckled at Joey's comment. Had it been anyone else calling Taj his baby, he would have smacked the teeth out of their mouth. "She is furious with a nigga. She refused to give me the grant and then put me out."

"Oh fuck," Joey grunted. "What's plan B?"

"Nigga, you know me. I never get to plan B. We still on plan A, I'm about to set some shit up right now."

"Don't let up on her. She'll hear you out, eventually," Joey assured. "You need her. Admit that shit to yourself out loud then admit it to her that you fucked up big time. Playa's fuck up all the time, the measure of the man is how he comes back."

The sound of Indigo sucking his teeth resounded through the receiver. "Nigga, who the fuck you been talking to in there?"

"Some OG's," Joey chuckled. "They been dropping jewels to a young nigga, cuh."

Indie laughed and sounded off again. "I've been dropping you jewels, nigga!"

"But you been gone for four years. I don't know you nigga," Joey joked. "I forgot all that shit."

"Shut up, cuh," Indie laughed.

Joey's laugh ceased and said, "Alright, I'll holla at you in a few days."

"Aight, lil' nigga. Stay up."

"Always."

Indie hung up the phone and tossed it on the bed. He placed his forearm against the window and leaned his head on it. The sun had fully come across the horizon. The city was beautiful. That was one thing he could also say about the Bay, it was beautiful. There was only one way to make this day better, Taj.

"Hey Siri," Indigo spoke up, waiting for his phone to wake up and follow his commands. "Call Maria."

Pulling himself away from the window, he took the phone off the bed and strolled to the bathroom of his hotel room.

Maria answered, "Hey, Indie."

"What's up girl? How are you doing?" Indie asked, splashing some water on his face. "Everything been good over there?"

Maria snorted with laughter before replying back, "Indie you know damn well everything ain't okay over here. She's not talking to me."

"Shit, that bad huh?" Indie ran his hand across his head. "My bad."

"It's no sweat, I'd do it again until she folds," Maria shared. "She's stubborn as fuck."

"Don't I know it," Indie grumbled. "She's a damn bull."

"But she's your bull and she misses you. So, tell me what I need to do to get this phase over with?" Maria asked.

"What's her schedule looking like tonight?" Indie questioned.

"She's done at three today...what are you thinking?"

Indie smirked softly like Maria could see him. "Set up

dinner at her favorite restaurant, I'll meet her there. Around five? I want to maximize our time."

"I got you," Marie's voice perked up. "You better come with the best game of your life. Real player shit."

"Always," Indie said with a smirk again. "I owe you."

"Nah, you don't owe me nothing but making Taj happy. It's been too long since she's had it..." Maria trailed off, realizing that she already said too much. Indie rose his brow and looked at the phone with his face twisted.

"What the hell is going on with her and that nigga?" Indie asked, cutting straight to the point.

Maria released a huff, then hummed, then sighed, and finally, she said, "I think you need to ask her about that."

Indie licked his bottom lip and thumbed the itch on the tip of his nose. "Aight, bet."

"I'll have everything set up," Maria assured. "You got this Indie. I'll be in touch."

Hanging up and running his hand down his face, "I hope so."

Chapter Sixteen

T aj

"MARIA, WHERE ARE YOU?" TAJ ASKED, WALKING INTO THE
restaurant with her phone pinned to her ear. "I could really be
home right now."

Maria's huff sounded off in Taj's ear, "Girl, you don't want
to be there anyway. I'll be there in a minute. I'm down the
street. Just go to the bar and order and drink, I'll be there in a
second."

"Alright, Maria," Taj spoke, rolling her eyes and headed
toward the bar. "Hurry up. If you're not here in ten minutes,
I'm going home."

"Girl," Maria huffed. "Bye."

She hung up and sauntered over to the bar and climbed in
the barstool. Her phone lit up with a notification from

Malcolm, just as she was about to flip it over. Glancing down at it, she quickly skimmed the message.

You should have been home by now...

"This nigga," Taj groaned, rubbing her temples before she waved down the bartender. "Could I get tequila and pineapple with salt around the rim and a lime?"

"Sure thing," the bartender nodded and started making her drink. "Long day?"

"Every day is a long day," Taj muttered, plowing her hair out of her face.

The bartender smirked and watched Taj type a message back to Maria before flipping her phone over.

"Let me lighten your load," a familiar voice crooned into her ear over her shoulder. "Mind if I take a seat?"

Taj cut her eyes over her shoulder and growled at the sight of Indie. "Didn't I tell you to leave me the fuck alone?"

Indie's voice rumbled with laughter and took a seat anyway. "You know I'm not going to do that. You've been ignoring my texts or having your little chihuahua intervene for you."

Taj rolled her eyes and retrieved her drink from the bartender. With three gulps, the drink was gone and she was waving him down for another. "Indigo, please."

"Indigo? We are back to that?" he asked with a soft smirk on his face that was bound to piss her off.

"You know what, I'm not doing this shit with you. I'm good," she spoke followed by a huff. Digging into her purse, she pulled out a few bills to cover her tab and slid off the barstool. Taj started her pursuit toward the door and Indie was right on her trail. Before she could hit the door, Indie gently grabbed her arm, making her wince lowly. She looked up at him with tears forming in her eyes. She easily got lost in Indie, that's how she ended up in this situation. Lost in him. Furious that she was lost in him. Livid that he let her stay lost in him for so long.

She grunted and snatched her arm away from him. "Don't touch me. Don't you dare touch me! You lost the right!"

As much as she didn't want to cause a scene in this restaurant, she couldn't stop her emotions from spewing over. Taj was tired of holding her feelings in for the sake of saving face. But as she looked up at Indie, she realized that she was out of control of her emotions.

"Baby, just let me talk to you. Give me five minutes." Indie followed her out of the restaurant onto the sidewalk. "Stop walking away from me."

"What do you want Indie! Huh? You want to waste more of my fucking time? Is this some sick ass game to you? You get off doing this shit!" Taj screamed up at him with a furrowed brow. A mixture of tears and snot streamed down her face. "Is that what you want! Huh? Indigo! Answer me!"

She shoved him backward with all of her might and he stumbled, throwing his hands up. "Answer me! All I did was love you! That's all I did in life and what I thought was death. I stopped living my life for you and you want to waltz back in and pick up where you left off! Nah nigga, nah. You don't get to break my heart twice."

Indie wanted to drop his head to escape Taj's sad face, but he couldn't. He did this to her. He took a step towards her and cupped her face. She pulled her face away and broke eye contact with him. The tears were pouring from her eyes and she couldn't stop crying. She needed to. She needed to release everything she was holding inside.

"I waited on you," she spoke between sobs. "I looked for you everywhere, just so I could function from day to day and you were here. Why did you leave me, Indie? What did I do to make you leave me?"

Indie's heart broke. He wrapped his arms around her and held her close to his chest. "What did I do?"

He kissed the top of her head through her curls and didn't care that they were in the middle of the sidewalk, having this conversation. He didn't care that people were watching in on their interaction. Nothing mattered but her.

"You didn't do anything," he muttered against her head. "I had to go, and I never thought I was going to be away from you this long. One thing led to another and before I knew it, years had gone by."

Taj pulled away from his and wiped her face. Carefully putting space between them, she analyzed him. Hearing his reasoning wasn't enough to satisfy the loneliness that his absence provoked. "That's not good enough for me."

Taj wrapped her arms around herself and started to shut down. "It's not enough...you wasted my fucking time."

She sniffled and looked around her surroundings, realizing that she just had a full-blown emotional break down in public. Wiping her face on her sleeves, she started to migrate up the sidewalk to her car. The breeze was hitting her face, bushing her back toward Indie as she fought so hard to get away.

Indie was hellbent on not letting her get away from him. He was right behind her. "Taj Ali Adams."

"Indie just let it go. It's done. It's over," she called over her shoulder.

"No," Indie based with a groan, making her stop in her tracks. "It's not over. I have thought about you every day for four years. I have prayed for you every day for four years. You think you're the only one walking around here refusing to move on, refusing to let go? You think you're the only one with a broken heart? You think I wanted to leave you?"

Taj slowly turned around to look at him. Watching his walk toward her with a slight limp, her heart sunk. *He must've got hit there too.* She thought to herself.

"I never wanted to leave you. You know I went to UCLA

after your classes started, just so I could see you. I came into town every so often just to check on you. I saw the pain in your eyes when you graduated."

"And still you were gone, what is that supposed to mean to me?" she shot out of spite. She instantly regretted it, seeing the anger flash in his eyes.

"Baby, they had a price on my head. Being with you made you a target too. Let me just talk to you and I'll tell you everything." He closed the gap and Taj put her hands up to stop him from getting too close.

With a shake of the head, she said, "I can't do that Indie."

"Is it because of that nigga?" Indie's envy of her returning home to another man spiked. "Just stay with me tonight Taj, so we can put everything out on the table."

"There is no table, Indie." Taj hummed and looked him up and down, taking a snapshot of how he looked now. "There is nothing to talk about."

Indie traced his bottom lip with his thumb and said, "Baby, I'll give you some time. But it won't be long until I see you again. That nigga you got at the house blowing your phone up, is a loaner, a place holder. You know where your heart is. You know what you want, what you need."

"Goodnight, Indie." She turned around and walked away to her car, climbed inside and sped off down the street. She was going to kill Maria for setting her up like this. But she didn't have the energy to deal with it or Malcolm.

Ugh, Malcolm.

Traveling from the parking garage to her condo, she inserted her key and walked into the house only to be met by Malcolm's glare of frustration. "Where the hell have you been?"

Taj frowned her face in disgust. "Back up."

Instead on conceding, Malcolm hovered over her. "He's still here isn't he, that's where you were?"

"You need to mind the business that pays you," Taj spoke up before pushing him out her way. "I ain't it."

She stormed past him and went to her room, locking the door and pressing her back against it, Taj let out a heavy sigh. She was emotionally spent. Part of her wished that she would have stayed with Indie to hear him out, but the other part of her wanted nothing to do with him and it was only because she was hurt. But how much longer could she ignore the feeling of needing him until it became unbearable.

Chapter Seventeen

R icky

"THE HOUSE HAS TWO MASTERS, THIS ONE AND ANOTHER one on the first level, great for guest," the realtor concluded the tour standing in the foyer between Indie, who towered over her and Ricky. She'd been flashing smiles at Indie since they arrived at the house. So much so that she'd ignored Ricky, who actually wanted to buy the house.

Ricky nodded his head and looked around. "I think she'll like it. Any other offers?"

"Just one, they're waiting on the bank," the realtor shared, looking at Ricky now that he was talking about money.

Nodding again, Ricky smirked, "I got cash. Throw my offer in the pot."

The realtor smiled and said, "I'll call them now. I'll be outside if you need me." Her comment was directed more toward Indie than Ricky. He shook his head and snorted with laughter. "Anything you need."

"I'm good love," Indie replied, not even giving her the satisfaction of looking down at her grin over her shoulder while she strutted to the door.

Ricky couldn't help but laugh at Indie's response. "Damn, next time I'm sending you to close. You got more juice than I do."

Indie rolled his eyes again and waved him off. "I'm not attracted to thirsty hoes."

"You know...if you weren't trying to get Taj back, I would say you were gay."

"You're short and you're annoying," Indie grumbled, clearly not in the best of moods. Ricky picked up that he hadn't been since he got back from San Francisco. He was inclined to ask him about the trip when we got back but seeing how Indie was in a rare form, he left it alone. But Ricky figured three days was enough to cool off and get himself together.

"Tell me something good," Ricky spoke up, standing in the middle of a house. He'd been eyeing this house close to a year. Before he only wished he had enough money to get it but now, he could buy it in cash and not bat an eye. Now that he had enough money for a real realtor to finally take him seriously enough to give him a tour, he wasn't leaving without it being his.

It wasn't too big and it sure wasn't as small as the one him and Ajai were currently living in. Dark wood floors were in every room of the house except the kitchen. The walls were painted white, but he was sure once Ajai had her way she would paint every wall in the house and bless it with her warm touch.

"I think this is going to be a dope ass gift to Ajai," Indie replied, ignoring the content behind Ricky's question. Indie started to roam through what was the living room, into the dining room and stopped in the kitchen. "I'm proud of you, cuh."

"Look, I don't like being shot in the damn hood I live in. Those niggas didn't even mean to shoot me...that's the crazy shit," Ricky spoke up followed by a snicker while he trailed Indie.

Indie scoffed. "Who you telling, I still got fragments in my leg."

"I like how we got off-topic, how was the Bay?" Ricky leaned against the counter and studied the troubled look pinned in Indie's brow. "That look on your face ain't good."

"She broke down. The shit that killed me was when she asked what did she do to make me leave her," Indie muttered, scratching his beard. "That shit tore me up. I want to give her space, but I really don't."

"Four years is enough space. She's stubborn as fuck though. Look at who her pops is...all she knows is how to be stubborn as fuck. You know how you used to pull up on her and force her out of the house? You got to pull up on her. Apply the pressure to make her drop that wall."

Indie nodded slowly. "Yeah, you're right. I got to get the nigga out the picture too. I don't trust shit about him."

"Don't nobody trust shit about him, cuh. Nobody but Senior. You apply enough pressure and make her yours or at least remind her about that old thing, he'll leave."

Indie hummed and shook his head. "I don't want to think about it right now. What else you got going on? It's been quiet out here."

"You would be on my head if it were loud nigga, just take what I give you," Ricky huffed.

"You better give me three duffle bags of cash and say, we done nigga, that's all I wanna hear when it comes to the streets," Indie spoke up. Ricky watched his expression go from grim to annoyed.

Ricky knew that Indie wanted nothing more than to be legit and Ricky wanted to make sure that they had enough when it happened. "I told you I had it. Let me do my thing."

"You know," Indie started back up with a chuckle and a wave of his finger in Ricky's direction. "Every time you have said that, some shit popped off. I'm going to let up off your neck but nigga, I swear if you're on some bullshit I'm coming for you."

Ricky kissed his teeth and waved Indie off. "Anyway, I didn't bring you here to talk about work or any of that shit. I brought you here to tell you that Ajai and I are getting married."

Indie's eyes shot out his head and a smile crept over his tense face, erasing the worry from his brows. "Say what, cuh?"

"Yeah, she been holding it down for a long time. Why not? We already solid. Marriage ain't gonna do nothing but add an official title to that shit." Ricky's comment made Indie's eyes flutter for a second. Ricky caught up and stopped talking. He looked at him and hummed.

"What?"

"How's your heart?" Ricky asked. "How are you feeling?"

"Honestly?" Indie questioned and Ricky nodded. "Like I'm on the verge of having everything I want and nothing at all."

"When you ride down the block and you look at everyone's faces, and you see the way they look back at you and their faces light up...you got more than you know, nigga. You got a city that loves you. You look in the mirror and you see Taj...listen to me. Stop fuckin' dragging your feet. Yeah, you fucked up, it's done. You're never going to be whole if you don't get your rib back. She'll be at the wedding in a couple of weeks. Make that shit count."

"Who are you?" Indie chuckled. "I got it. I'm going to take care of it. Just one of them days nigga."

"We all got them. Remember Jermaine used to say, the measure of the man ain't how he falls..."

"It's how he gets his black ass up and make the shit shake," Indie finished Ricky's statement. "Aight, let's get out of here. I'm hungry and I got to check on the office buildings."

Ricky watched as Indie walked out of the kitchen toward the front door where the realtor was standing on the phone. He looked away from Indie and looked around the house, smirking lightly, he nodded his head. Soon enough the house was to be full of their family and friends, celebrating their official union. He was excited to start his new chapter with Ajai. He owed her everything, outside of his mom and Indie, she held him down and set him straight. Ricky could only pray that Indie felt this feeling again. The feeling of completeness.

After they ate, checked on the properties, Ricky dropped Indie off and headed to his moms to pick up Bleu. Instead of going inside immediately, Ricky got out of the car and pulled his phone out of his pocket. He sat on the stairs and hit Taj's name. The call went to voicemail but Ricky wasn't letting her off the hook that easily. Calling again, he repositioned his arm in the sling and winced.

"What do you want?" she questioned. Ricky drew his neck back and pulled the phone away from his ear to make sure his ears weren't bleeding.

"Got damn girl. What happened to the good ol fashioned hello?" Ricky teased.

Taj grunted and he could feel her attitude course through the phone. "Same thing that happened to being truthful."

"Baby," he countered with a sigh. "I couldn't."

"Nah, you wouldn't"

"My loyalty –"

"Lied with Indie...of course it did." Taj cut him off before she said something to herself under her breath. Ricky wasn't even going to strain his ears to hear her because he knew that Taj would say what she was thinking eventually. "You know, what. I'm not even mad at you. If I could be real, I feel stupid for believing that my family would have my back. But I guess it's not as solid as I thought it was."

"I would rather let you be mad at me than keep taking it out on Indie. Yeah, he fucked up, but the nigga got his reason's Baby. He's not right without you. He hasn't been himself in years," Ricky continued to defend Indie. Taj huffed in his ear.

"You know it's okay, Ricky. I'm going to move on, and he can too." Her response made him jolt to his feet.

"Move on with the bum-ass nigga. I think the fuck not. You know Bubba would not allow that shit, Baby. We don't allow that shit. I don't trust shit about him," Ricky damn near shouted.

"You don't have to trust nothing. Don't even use that word with me. Trust is out the wind --"

"So, you're going to just throw away everything for that bitch you sleeping with it?" Ricky's pressure was high.

"Ricky," Taj let off her lips in a warning tone.

"Don't Ricky me, Baby. Tell me he ain't one. He's a bitch nigga, that nigga don't have no sort of code. I've gotten rid of niggas like him. Fuck him and fuck his momma, Baby. You're holding on to him because that shit is comfortable...but does it feel good? Answer that. Are you happy?"

Taj grew quiet and Ricky grunted knowing the truth.

"I'm not doing this Ricky."

"Because you know I'm right. You know where you need to be. Stop being so got damn stubborn and come home. Hear him out, he's trying so hard, Baby. He's fighting shit every day that he don't talk about. But I know, I see it on his face. He needs you and you need him. This shit has got to end, it's gone on long enough."

Ricky could hear Taj sniffle and try to breathe through her emotion. "I run the risk of losing him again. Why would I want to put myself through that twice? Who wants to go through having their heart ripped out twice? There is no secret that I loved him...that I still love him. I've never loved anyone before him, and it has been hell to love someone after him."

"You know where your heart is at...just go back to it and stop this mess. It's a fuckin' mess. Honestly, he looks fuckin' pitiful"

"I'll talk to you later, Ricky. I love you," Taj spoke after growing quiet again for almost a minute.

"I love you too. Always. And if I need to come up there and fuck the bitch ass nigga up. I will."

"Bye, Ricky," Taj rumbled softly before hanging up.

He hung up and stared at the screen for a second. He missed her. Who she was before everything took place. Ricky understood that Taj would never be the same but to see her be remotely close to who she was, would be wonderful. If he really thought about it, none of them were the same. They saw so much, been through even more and all of that pain showed on their faces, in their body language, and in their actions. It hit Ricky like a ton of bricks. He finally felt what Indie had been preaching all of those years. The hood would change you, eat you, and spit you out. However, you came out on the other end was all up to you.

With a grunt, Ricky pushed himself to his feet and traveled inside to share the good news of his engagement with his mother. Every day since getting shot, he would come over and show her his face so she wouldn't worry about whether or not he was safe.

"Hey Ma," he softly greeted, easing his way into the house.

He was sure not to make too much noise, in the event that Bleu was sleep. "What you got going on?"

Mary was sitting on the couch with Bleu sleeping on her lap. Ricky appreciated that; unlike some grandparents she kept him on his schedule, instead of letting him run around like he ruled the world. "I see you learned your lesson for last time."

Ricky laughed softly and eased down on the couch by her after securing the front door. "I can still feel that pop upside the head."

"Good, maybe I should have popped you more as a child," she replied in a hushed tone. "How's your arm doing?"

"It's cool...hurt sometimes but I got lucky." Ricky readjusted his arm and winced slightly. "You know you got a little wedding to come to in about two weeks."

Mary popped her brow upward and looked over her son like he was speaking a language that was foreign to her. "A wedding? Who's getting married. I know it ain't you."

"Ma you only have one child who can get married," Ricky countered, rolling his eyes. "We're getting married, Ma. Nothing big, just us, Indie, Diane...Senior."

Ricky couldn't help but groan when he said Senior's name. "Hopefully Taj."

"Oh yeah, where is this little wedding supposed to be taking place?" Mary continued with her questions.

"At our house."

"Well excuse me. Getting shot straightened you out some huh?" she chuckled lightly after her comment. Now fully looking at him, he squirmed.

"What do you mean, some?"

Mary smacked her lips and let a huff escape. "I'm wasn't born yesterday boy. I know what you're up to. I saw Manny come over the other day before you got shot. According to previous conversations, y'all were supposed to be drying out...seems like you still have a river running. My question is, are you ready for the consequences of it?"

"What you mean, ain't nobody going to do nothing to me," Ricky curled his lip at the thought of a nigga on the street running up on him behind some work.

"There's only one person who can touch you...be prepared for that interaction," Mary warned before changing her tone. "As far as the wedding. I will be there."

Ricky let her warning go in one ear and out the other. "We got an extra room if you want to move in."

"Thank you but that's not necessary son. I've lived here all my life and I'm fine. You and Ajai need your space."

"Aight ma," Ricky replied, leaning his head back and resting it on the cushions. Closing his eyes, he grew quiet, relaxed, and drifted off to sleep.

Untitled

Please stay from 'round me
'Cause I know how I'll be
Lost til you found me
Girl, I lose all composure
All you gotta say is go
Then we losing control
August Alsina: Control

Chapter Eighteen

jai

A WEEK HAD PASSED SINCE RICKY SHARED THE NEWS OF them moving out of the hood. Excitement coursed through Ajai. She was enrolled back into school; she was moving into a new home out of the hood and her and Ricky were about to walk hand-in-hand for the rest of their life. She ran her eyes over the small list of guests, who were going to share this moment with them, and they'd all promised to be there but one. Taj.

After hearing about the meltdown, she had when Indie popped up on her, Ajai hesitated about having them in the same room. Ajai wanted to keep her feelings in mind but after everything was said and done, it was her day, and everyone needed to act right so she could enjoy her day. Taj would just have to put herself to the side for a few hours.

Picking up her phone and hitting Taj's name, Ajai waited for her to pick up. It rung a few times before she answered, "Hey Ajai."

"Hey girl," Ajai spoke up with a smile widening her lips. "How are you?"

"You know, every day above ground is a blessing," Taj replied. It was almost like she rehearsed it to convince herself and there was an underlying tone of sarcasm. "What's going on?"

"Soooo," Ajai started up again, ignoring Taj's last comment because she didn't know how to take it. "Ricky and I are getting married and I would love if you would come."

"Married? Wow, that's amazing," Taj voice perked up with genuine happiness.

Ajai's smile grew wider, hearing the happiness in Taj's voice. "I don't know if him getting shot shook some sense into him but –"

"Wait, shot..."

"He got hit by a stray bullet, how ironic is that?" Ajai asked, hearing Taj chuckle a bit.

"Well, thank God it wasn't intentional, I could only imagine how they would have handled that," Taj released.

"Exactly, it just hit him in the arm but you know your cousin is a baby."

"He's your baby," Taj added. "Listen, I would love to come but..."

Ajai groaned and massaged her temples. "Taj...don't give me any bullshit okay? Leave Maleficent at home and come be with your family. I'm not taking no as an answer. I miss you."

Taj chuckled at Ajai referral to Malcolm but still hesitated to answer, Ajai could feel it. "Okay... only for a day. I'll fly in the day of and fly out the day after."

"Whatever you have to do as long as you're there in a pretty dress and a smile on your face. It won't be big at all. Just a small ceremony and family dinner afterward."

"Alright, Ajai. I'd hate myself if I missed this."

"I know you would," Ajai replied in a sing-along tone. "I'll see you in a week?"

"You have my word, I'll be there."

"You'll be alone?"

Taj scoffed softly with a laugh to follow. "Yes, I will be there in a week, in a pretty dress, a smile on my face, and alone."

"Perfect. I'll see you soon."

Saying their goodbyes, Ajai hung up and went back to packing up the remainder of the house. Indie, Manny, and Rico had moved all the big things that Ricky couldn't. She was grateful for them because there was no way she was going to be doing everything alone.

While she packed up the small things, her mind flashed back on how they felt when they moved into this house. It was a few months after Indie slipped out of the city and Ricky's heart was heavy. There were nights she would find him sitting in Indie's room, staring at the wall. There days where he would say it should have been him. All of it made her fearful.

Ricky was already a hot head by nature, and she didn't know how bad off he would be without Indigo to calm him down. She found herself taking on the role of being his voice of reason, but she knew she could never replace Indie. Even when Ricky started to become his own man without relying on Indie. She could still see without his brother and his best friend; he was lost at sea looking for his way home. He wasn't fully out of the streets yet, and Ajai knew that Ricky would take his sweet ass time, but something was better than nothing.

Moving out of this house was a sure sign that they were well on their way to a better tomorrow. Ricky's face held traces of hope again. She hadn't seen that in a while. And now that she finally had her man on track, she could only hope that Indie found his way back to what kept him going all of those years.

Looking over her shoulder at Indie wandering back into the house, she smirked. "Taj will be here next week."

"Oh yeah?" Indie asked, picking up a box. "She coming by herself or..."

"Alone because I don't want any shit on my wedding day," Ajai pointed out. "This is your last chance to get the girl of your dreams back."

Indie shifted like he didn't want to talk about it or her but Ajai was sick of the back and forth. "I know you're not the man to make her come to you...but you need to show her you want her back."

"You're right. I've never been that nigga. I'd rather her come back because she wants to, not because I forced her to. I will not make nobody love me and I damn sure ain't about to put my foot on her neck. What I need is for her to understand why I did what I did. If she wants to move forward it would be love, if not...I get it."

"Well for the sake of staying optimistic let's say she decides to move forward what's the next move?" Ajai turned fully around to face him and place her hand on her hip. "Because I'm sick of this shit. Y'all got my damn head spinning around."

Indie chuckled. "What you mean what's the next move. If she's down to move forward, I ain't wasting time. I'm a peaceful type of nigga, but at the end of the day...she's mine. Always was and always will be. She ain't leaving here without knowing that."

"That's that shit I like!" Ajai grinned so big, her eyes disappeared behind her cheeks. "I got faith in you. I talked to her. She doesn't sound as mad as she was so hopefully the universe is working in your favor."

"Everything that's supposed to be, will be," Indie replied with a flash of light in his eyes that Ajai hadn't seen. Her heart skipped a beat. She wanted to point it out, but she was going to leave it alone. Everything was so close to falling back into place. Everything was starting to align in their favor.

"You know...I'm proud of you. It takes a big man to admit he's wrong and to try to fix it."

"I'm not above saying I dropped the ball," he replied with a shrug. "I'm just trying to get right."

"Well keep it up because it's rubbing off on Ricky," Ajai spoke up with a light giggle. "Please keep it up."

"Ay, you know Ricky is a two-person job. I can't keep him straight without help," Indie said. "It takes a village to raise a son right."

Ajai laughed as Ricky walked in the door. "You in here keke-ing with my girl, cuh? Get your own and come on!"

Indie cut his eye at Ajai and laughed again. "Nigga, you really got to calm down. I'm about to make you move the rest of this shit by yourself."

"I wish you would," Ricky grunted.

Indie laughed him off. "For someone with a sling, you talk a lot of shit. All it takes is me ripping that Velcro off, for you to remember who the fuck you talking to."

"Alright girls! You're both pretty, move the boxes please," Ajai huffed, rolling her eyes at the two. "Quit it."

"You lucky my girl's here. I'm not going to show out in front of her," Ricky teased, making Indie snort.

"It ain't like she ain't never seen you show your ass for less, nigga."

Chapter Nineteen

❧

M aria

"WHAT ABOUT THIS DRESS?" MARIA ASKED TAJ, WHO WAS seated in the middle of the closet with her butt resting on her bottom of her feet. "It's cute for the wedding."

Taj shook her head. "It's too frilly."

"What about this one?" Mari pulled out another dress with yellow flowers printed all over it. The way Taj's face frowned prompted Maria to put the dress back in its spot. "Girl. we've been doing this for almost an hour now. What do you want to wear?"

"Nothing, because I don't want to go," Taj mumbled, folding a UCLA t-shirt and placing it inside of her duffle bag.

Maria pulled out a slinky spaghetti-strapped blue dress and admired it. While Taj was distracted folding a few leggings and t-shirts, she slipped it into her garment bag with a pair of strappy silver heels. Dropping to her knees, she started helping Taj sift the pile of clothes on the floor. "Why don't you want to go?"

Taj pursed her lips together and shot Maria look. Quickly nodding her head and smirked, she fell back on her butt and said, "You cannot run from him forever. You and I both know how much you love him. So, you got your second chance finally. Take it and don't look back."

"It's so much easier said than done," Taj shared, stuffing the remainder of the clothes in the bag. "I've talked myself out of going three times already. But I know Ajai is going to cuss me out if I don't go."

Maria rolled her eyes heavily. She loved Taj there was no doubt about it, but Taj was dragging this out a lot longer than she needed to. It was insane to Maria why Taj didn't run at the opportunity of having Indie back. She'd been trying to save her questions for when she thought that Taj was ready to answer but there wasn't any better time than now to ask her. Especially while they were alone, and Malcolm wasn't lurking around corners.

"Something is on your mind, I can feel it," Taj spoke up, sensing that Maria had questions burning to be released from her throat without even looking at her. "Go ahead and ask me whatever is burning to be released."

Maria blew her hair out her face and zeroed in on Taj. "What's holding you back? Is it because of Malcolm?"

Taj huffed, rested her hands in her lap and stared down at them. "Partially...you got to understand that up until recently Malcolm was everything that a woman wanted. He was kind and considerate. I didn't have to ask for anything and ulti-mately, he was there for me even when I made it so fucking difficult for him to be. So, leaving him, after years, isn't the easiest thing for me to do. Because although Indie is my home, he's where my heart lives...Malcolm is my house. I don't love it, but I live there, and I've filled it with things."

"But a house isn't a home, Taj," Maria replied, and Taj nodded her head.

"I know. But I've lost Indie once. The risk of loving him is high, the risk of losing him and not being able to bounce back from that loss is higher. Trust me it has taken everything in me not to say fuck this, I'm going home."

Just as Maria was going to open her mouth to reply, Malcolm pushed the door of the closet open. It was clear that he'd been drinking. The smell of whiskey greeted them before he did. "Where the fuck are you going?"

Maria pinched her nose and pinned her brows together. "First of all, Malcolm...it's noon and you're drunk."

Malcolm curled his lip and shot Maria a look that made her mirror his expression. "Where are you going?"

He asked the question again, this time as if Maria nor Taj could hear him before. With a slight roll of the eyes, Maria was ready to tell him where he could go and how fast he could get there. But out of respect for Taj and her home, she would let her handle her man.

Taj stood up and grabbed a pair of shoes off the shelf and placed them in a separate bag. "I'm going to Los Angeles, Malcolm."

If his face twisted anymore it would have broken. Malcolm grunted in disgust. Maria studied how easily he was unraveling at the mention of Taj leaving for a weekend. "I'm coming with you."

"No, it's best that you stay here," Taj's voice was even but Maria still wasn't liking how this conversation was going. She stood to her feet and positioned herself against the tiny dresser just in case Malcolm wanted to catch a pair of free hands.

Malcolm's lip curled to the point his lips were tight and

wrinkled. "Stay...here...and let you go to L.A. to see that dirty ass nigga. You're out your fucking mind. You ain't going. Unpack that shit."

"Woah who are you talking to?" Maria's voice rose a few levels as she studied him with her brows pinched. "You out your mind talking to her crazy like that."

Once again, Malcolm cut his eyes at her. "You are in my house."

"Aht!" Maria threw up her hand. "This is Taj's house. She pays the bills in here, too. You're just here..."

"Maria," Taj groaned as she bit on her lip and caught Malcolm's glare. "Can you just give us a minute?"

"You sure?" Maria, asked not budging and keeping her eyes on Malcolm. "You'll be good?"

"I'll be fine." Taj watched as Maria walked past her and out of the room.

"I'll be right here in case he wants his top peeled back!" Maria called from the living room.

Taj

MALCOLM WAITED UNTIL MARIA WAS OUT OF SIGHT TO close the closest door and stalk toward Taj. She tried her best to hold face and not let him see that she was terrified of him. Flashing back on her conversation, she was justified. Up until recently, Malcolm had the potential of her closing the door on Indie and moving on with him. But he was possessed by jealousy and couldn't keep his hands to himself or control on his liquor.

He'd left marks on her forearms and wrist from his grip alone and still, Taj tried to give him a pass. Covering up her arms to be sure that no one saw them, but she was growing tired quickly and this wasn't what she signed up for. But Malcolm had Senior's approval and if he hid Indie from her for four years, he would probably turn a blind eye to Malcolm's behavior.

"So, this is your house now? Huh?" he questioned. "You pay the bills in this bitch now?"

"Stop it and open the door," Taj whispered. "I am not doing this with you today. My flight leaves in an hour."

"I look like I care about that flight?" he growled at her. "Look at me? Does it look like I give a fuck?"

"Malcolm," Taj struggled to find her voice as she watched him close in on her. "I'm going to L.A. and I'll be back on Monday. That's all there is to it."

"I'm supposed to believe this you're going for some wedding?" Malcolm gnashed his teeth at her with flared nostrils. "For all, I know you could be going to fuck that nigga. Since you've been calling out his name and shit."

"Take a step back," Taj ordered, attempting to ward him off with her tiny hands. "Get away from me."

Malcolm ignored her pleads and boxed her in. He pinned her body to the wall with his and slammed his hands against the wall making her jump a bit. "Please move."

"You fuck him, and I swear there will be hell to pay." He grabbed her chin roughly and forced her to look at him. "I'm the one that's been tiptoeing around you, picking up after you, making sure you got everything you fucking need while you ignored me and moped around. That was me. You remember that shit you hear me...remember that. He will leave you again and I will not be the fool that sticks around waiting on you. Have your ass back here on Monday, or I promise you."

"You promise what?" Maria questioned, forcefully pushing the door open with a knife in her hand.

Malcolm quickly let go of Taj's face and took a step back. "That's what I thought nigga," Maria grunted. "That's exactly what the fuck I thought. Taj get your bags and let's go. You have a flight to catch and a wedding to attend."

"Ali, remember what I told you," Malcolm grumbled, walking past Maria while looking over his shoulder.

"You ain't her damn daddy! She doesn't have to remember shit you say about shit. Get your ass out of here!" Maria barked at him. "Come on Taj before you miss this flight."

Taj had held herself together after the encounter with Malcolm. She got herself ready, blinked any tears she had in her eyes away, and put a little bit of foundation on her face to cover up any potential marks he left behind.

The ride to the airport was quiet. Maria was fuming but Taj just stared into her phone, consumed with her emails and going through the investments she wanted to award. Indie's name was still on the list with an asterisk beside it. She didn't have the heart to remove it completely yet. Nor did she have the heart to shut down his dream. Who was she kidding? This was Indigo Sims; when it came to his dreams no one could stand in the way of them, not even her.

"You're not going to talk about what I saw back there?" Maria broke the silence.

"No..." Taj shot back. "We won't...and if I thought that we were I would have taken an Uber."

Maria smacked her lips and huffed. "How many times has he put his hands on you, Taj?"

"Maria," Taj dragged out in annoyance. "I just said I didn't want to talk about it. I don't want to talk about it. It's not going to change anything. When I get back, he will still be there, and I will still have to deal with his fucking attitude. I don't want to talk about it, I don't want to think about it."

Maria pressed his lips together and squinted her eyes.

"Fine, but when you're ready to talk about it. I'll listen because I love you and if you need me to stab him, I will because I love you."

"I know you do," Taj almost whispered.

"Don't leave L.A. without making a decision...this right here ain't the way you're supposed to be living."

Taj cut her a look that didn't faze her. Maria shrugged her shoulders and turned into the airport drop off. "I'm just saying."

"Mmhmm. I'll call you when I'm getting ready to come back. I love you."

"I love you, too."

Maria blew Taj a kiss as she gathered her things and headed into the airport. Now that she was away from Maria, she could drop the act for a moment. Her heart sank and wanted to run away from everything, but it wouldn't solve anything. Instead, she scrambled to get to her terminal before the gates closed. Once she was checked and, in her seat, she sent Maria a quick text and melted into her seat.

Placing her AirPods into her ears, she hummed to herself. "Whatever is for you, Taj, will be yours. Just let the shit happen."

Soon it was wheels up and she couldn't turn around now. She was flying into her future and had to stop fighting it.

Chapter Twenty

I ndigo

THE CEREMONY HAD COME AND GONE, AND INDIE HADN'T taken his eyes off of Taj. The navy-blue dress Maria packed for her, clung to her body just enough to make him jealous of the fabric. When she walked in earlier alone, he thought it would be easy to keep it cordial with her. Up until now, he'd been doing a great job with it. He caught her eye earlier in the day, she flashed him a tiny smile, nodded her head and continued like they were just associates. Although that small gesture didn't work well for him, he was determined to keep his distance until later. He barely got through dinner across the table from her. Ricky had already warned him about causing a scene, so he kept what was bubbling inside of him, on the inside. But now the music was playing, and everyone was dancing. Ricky and Ajai were engulfed in each other, along with the other couples.

Indigo coolly sat back in his chair, sipping his drink while he watched Taj on the other side of the room peck away at her phone. Every so often she would take a moment to sip from her glass, look around the room and then back at her phone. He assumed she was doing work and not checking in with that nigga she left at home. His eyes traced her, landing on the ring on her finger. It made him cringe. That would be the first thing he took off if given the opportunity.

"Are you going to stare at her all night or ask her to dance?" Diane's voice sounded off softly in her son's ear before she could take a seat by him. "You've been staring at her since she walked through the door. What are you waiting for? It's getting creepy now."

Indie pulled his eyes off of Taj and placed them on his mother who stood on his right side. "The better question is why aren't you out there?"

"Because my dance partner is away right now," Diane answered his question with a glimpse of sadness in her eyes. Indie studied his mother's face and couldn't help but feel responsible for Joey's current situation. One thing Joey took pride in was putting a smile on their mother's face.

"You know just because he's not here doesn't mean you can't dance. I got you," Indie mumbled, standing up and taking his mother by the hand. "Come on girl, with your fine self."

Making their way to the dancefloor, Indie placed his hand in the small of her back and danced with her through a few songs. They sang along with the lyrics of Candy Coated Raindrops. When it came down the women Indie loved it didn't matter who was around, he would do whatever he needed to do to keep a smile on their faces. If it was singing Candy Coated

Rain Drops and doing a two-step with his mother to see her light up, he was going to do it.

"Your father used to sing this song to me," she muttered, letting her smile fade as the DJ switched up the song.

"Do you still miss that nigga?" Indie asked with a curl of the lip. His father wasn't someone he gave much thought to. He had several chances to reconnect with his kids, but he failed.

"No. We had good times though before they went bad. I will never hate him though, he gave me you and Joey," Diane shared. "You two have his face so I could never miss him, y'all haven't given me a chance to."

Indie rolled his eyes slightly and pursed his lips. "Enough of talking about him."

"Not yet. I know you're not your father, nor do I ever want you to take for granted what you have..." Diane's voice trailed off as his attention was taken back and held by Taj. She'd gotten up to get another drink and for a moment, she wasn't focused on her phone. Indie watched as Mary grabbed her by the hand and pulled her to the dance floor. If Taj could have fought her aunt off and returned back to her corner, she would have. But instead, her face flushed bright red with aggravation.

"Baby, I am not going to let you sit in that corner and drink the night away," Mary's voice rang out loud enough for Indie to hear. "You're young and beautiful. You can work tomorrow."

"Ugh, auntie," Taj groaned while Mary placed her hands-on Taj's hips, forcing them to move left and right. "I don't dance."

"You should start," Mary returned, still making Taj's stiff body move. Taj couldn't fight the smile and the fit of giggles she was about to be thrown into while Mary danced around her. "Just feel the beat and move them hips."

Mary was moving Taj closer to Indie with her dance moves. The more Taj danced, the more her wall was dropped and her hair was falling down. Indie couldn't help but smile at the way Taj's eyes lit up when she found her groove. It didn't take Mary long before accidentally bumping into Indie.

"Oh, I'm sorry, Indie," Mary apologized breathlessly, finally putting a pause to her dancing. "I didn't see you there."

Indie chuckled, knowing that Mary meant to do it. "It's all good Ms. Mary. I know short people don't normally look up."

"And giants normally don't look down," Mary shot back after taking a moment to breathe. "You look nice, though."

"He cleans up nice," Diane replied with a smile fixing, the lapels on Indigo's suit jacket before laying her eyes on Taj. "Taj you look beautiful."

Taj's eyes met with Indie's and didn't break away. Even though he was sure she wanted to pull them away. His heart fluttered like it was the first time he laid eyes on her.

"Diane, I'm too old to be out here shaking my ass with these kids," Mary spoke up, watching Indie and Taj become entranced with one another. "Let's get a drink and let these two have a moment."

Diane released Indie and he didn't even notice that she'd stepped away from him. Everyone in the room had disappeared.

"Hi," Taj finally spoke up. "I'm going to go..."

Indie knew that she didn't want to go, and he wasn't in the mood to prolong this anymore. She started to walk away but Indie caught her hand and pulled her back. Taj didn't fight him which surprised him. But he knew that at any moment, she could pull away and leave the party so he was going to make this moment last as long as he could. Her body melted into his as they swayed back and forth to the music. No one initiated the movement, it just happened like their bodies were still in sync with each other. Her scent took over his nostrils, making his grip tighten around her waist. He craned his neck down to press his lips against her ear and mutter. "I'm sorry."

Taj pulled away from him slightly and looked at him with tears cradled in the brim of her eyes. He could sense the fear that she tried to hide behind her wall, but he could see it and feel it.

"I don't want to do this here," she muttered, trying to hold herself together. "Not right now. I'm not going to ruin their day."

"Then when?" Indie asked, studying every line on her face.

"Later...I leave in the morning." Taj informed him with a sigh and took custody of her hands from his before pushing her hair behind her ears. "I don't think we should..."

Indie shook his head and pulled him back to her. Pressing his ear against her ear again, his growl was low and seductive. "You're not leaving tomorrow. You're not leaving me until this is fixed."

Taj tried her best not to pull her lips between her teeth and give in to him. He felt it. The heat radiating from her. Her body tightening at the core and begging for him to do right by it again. It – she – needed his attention, his tender touch, his gentle care. He knew it. It was written in the lines of her face. Her body exuded it like her sweet perfume in his nostrils.

Taj traced her bottom lip with the tip of her tongue and replied, "I'm not doing this here with you, right now. If you want this to be fixed, we'll do it later."

"We're doing this now. Go get your things," he ordered before placing a soft kiss to the curve of her jawline.

Taj flushed red, quickly looking around to see if anyone was watching him take full control of this situation. Luckily, everyone else was busy with their own thing. That gave her the ammunition she needed to pull away from Indie, get her clutch and her phone, and follow him out to his car.

Indie pulled the door of his brand new navy blue Audi open and let her slide inside. It wasn't long before they were pulling onto the interstate heading toward the hotel where Taj was staying for the night. He'd overheard the conversation at dinner about where she was staying and why she wasn't staying with Mary. Indie knew the reason she opted to stay in the city was so Senior couldn't get to her so easily.

Indie parked the car in the hotel parking lot, but Taj was eyeing the waves crash against the shore just a few feet away. Indie didn't need her to say what she wanted; he was still connected to her and he could pick up on it in an instant. Swinging his long legs out the car, Indie made his way over to the passenger side to open the door for her.

"Come on, let's take a walk," he coaxed her out of the car.

Hand-in-hand, the two walked down to the beach. Before Taj's feet could hit the sand, Indie kneeled down to removed her feet from her heels.

"Thank you," Taj softly spoke, looking down at him unstrap her heels. Placing her hand on his shoulder to steady her, Indie looked up at her and smirked.

"No need to thank me, Baby," he rumbled, standing up. He took her hand back into his and help her shoes in the others. They continued their walk for another five minutes before she broke the silence around them. "Tell me why...I need to know."

Indie stopped and turned to face her. The wind was causing her hair to dance around her face and moon illuminated the look on her face. Her brows creased in the middle, her mouth was fixed in a pout and her eyes were full of wonder. Indie took a second to admire the softness that consumed her. It was a one-eighty from the Taj he'd been dealing with previously.

He scratched his chin through the hair of his beard before answering her. "Everything that happened that night was out of my control. I didn't know that someone wanted me dead. All I knew was I needed to protect you, even if meant I had to do it with my life. I promised you I would protect you and that's what I did. When everything was said and done, it was easier for me to leave than stay around. And to tell you the truth, I never meant to hurt you. Knowing that I did has torn me up for four years. I'm not afraid to say I fucked up. Big time. I'm here now and I'm not asking you to pick up where we left off because that's impossible. You're a different woman and I'm a different man. But even with that, I've never stopped loving you. All I ask is that you allow me to know that new woman." Indie's answer was honest, his intentions with her were still pure.

He closed the space between them and stroked her cheek, removing the one tear she let fall.

"How am I supposed to know you won't leave me again? That this is safe to move forward with?"

"Baby, you know just like I know that probably as long as I have air in my body, I will never be safe. But I will be yours and you'll be home. I need you to come home."

Taj pulled away and took her lip between her teeth. "Home?"

"Home. Where you were always supposed to be. And don't tell me no, because I know..."

"You don't know me, Indie." Taj's protest fell on deaf ears. Indie wasn't going to let up now that he had her where he wanted her. He wasn't going to let up.

He chuckled and let his thick tongue lick his lips. "I know you enough to know that you will try to fight me because the control you finally feel, you don't want to let it go."

He took another step to her to close the gap even more. "I know that you've prayed to God for me...I know that you don't love that nigga you're wastin' your time with. I know that you love me. I know it won't let up off you."

"You don't know me, Indigo. I've changed," Taj continued to protest, trying to convince herself more than him.

Indie thought it was cute. He smirked and traced his eyes over her body. "Oh yeah?"

"Yeah..." she returned, shifting under his gaze.

"I know you won't run into the ocean in your dress and get your hair wet. Because whoever you are now cares about her cookie-cutter image." He could coax a snake not to bite. "This Taj probably hasn't laughed or let her hair down in years."

Taj smacked her lips, dropped her eyes from his and turned around to walk away from him. The closer she got to the shore, the more the smile she was trying to hold unleashed itself and took over her being. Indie count help but smirk, watching her make well on the bet he silently made with her.

Removing the jacket to his suit and his shoes, he followed behind her to be sure that she didn't get swept away by a wave. Taj traveled deep into the water until it came up to her stomach and turned around to see Indie approaching with a rumble of laughter escaping his lips.

"I thought for sure you were going to call my bluff." He reached her and pulled her into him.

"Anything else you know I won't do?" Taj sassed, only for Indie to gently lift her chin.

"This," he brushed his lips against hers before pulling her lips into his. "You won't pull away either."

Taj automatically wrapped her arms around his waist, letting Indie's lips fuse into hers. While his tongue massaged hers, she moaned lightly into his mouth. Indie held her closer. The waves continued to push against them swaying then back and forth, neither of them was fazed by it. Indie's hands found their temporary home on her ass.

They were intoxicated off the kiss alone. The salty taste from the water and the breeze and the liquor they consumed during the night was creating ecstasy. Their flames that were low, were building into a larger flame and their touch was electric. There wasn't a doubt in Indie's mind that this was where Taj belonged.

Taj pulled away and looked up at his hooded eyes. "Do you know that I can't go another day without you?"

"I know," he spoke softly, like it was their secret to keep. "Say what you need I got you."

Taj reached up and traced his face with her fingertips. She didn't say anything. Although Indie knew what she wanted next, he needed to hear it from her.

"I need love...real love...that I feel all over my body. The love that when you're gone, I still lean my body toward you...I need you."

"I'm yours."

"All of you. Withholding nothing from me. Honesty, protect my heart. I know what it is to live without you, I don't want to ever be there again. I just need you."

Indie took her hand kissed the tips of her fingers. "It's yours. Anything else?"

Taj nodded her head, hoping that he would say it for her. "Tell me what you want, Taj."

"I want you. I want to feel you. I need you to stay the night."

"You want a cuddle and talk about the past or you want a nigga to remind you how security and good dick feels?" Indie questioned.

Taj ran her hands from his face to his chest. "Remind me of how good you feel."

"Let's go."

Chapter Twenty-One

※◈※

T aj

THEY WEREN'T FULLY INSIDE OF HER HOTEL ROOM YET before Indie's mouth connected with her flesh, his hands gently resting on the base of her neck. Taj stumbled backward, dropping Indie's jacket that was draped over her shoulders, and their shoes on the floor. Indie wrapped his arms around her waist to support her before he kicked the door shut with his foot. Taj held on to him welcoming his lips and the trace of his tongue from her mouth to her neck, her collar bone, her shoulders until they ran over her left hand. Indie removed the diamond ring and tossed it across the room.

"I don't want to see that shit."

The room was only lit by the light creeping through the shades that were partially shut. It graced and highlighted the parts of her flesh she wanted him to kiss next. Hooking his fingers in the straps of her wet dress, he peeled it off her shoulders and off her body. He took a moment to step back as she stepped out of it. Taj opted out wearing a bra with the dress but the lace thong made his mouth water. He bit his lip and grunted.

Taj stepped toward him and started to unbutton his dress shirt. After every button was undone, she pushed it off his shoulders and traced her fingers over his scars. Every scar was caressed by her lips, all the while undoing his belt. These scars represented how strong he was to her. How he shielded her, how much he loved her.

Indie's dress pants fell to the floor and his boxer briefs was soon to follow.

"Thank you," Taj hummed seductively, wrapping her hand around his dick and massaging it. "For loving me enough to put everything on the line."

Just as Indie was going to respond, Taj dropped to her knees and swallowed him whole. "Got damn, baby."

Placing her hands on his hips to steady herself, she slurped, moaned, and pleased him like she would never get another chance to show him how thankful she was for him. Spit dripped from the corners of her mouth and off the tip of his dick, she smiled and admired how beautiful it was. His grunts were proof that she was doing a great job thanking him. "Shit...baby."

Taj placed a couple kissed to the head of his dick before taking it back in her mouth. Indie's hands gripped the root of her hair, allowing her to move her hand from his hips down between her thighs. The heat that radiated from between her thighs made her moan but not more than discovering how wet she was. Sucking his dick had aroused her more than she assumed it would. While he panted, curled his toes and pulled her head back and forth, she split her lips and massaged her pearl with her middle finger. Dipping the finger inside of her every so often, she moaned.

Indie winced and pulled himself from between her cheeks, "I'm not ready to bust yet, baby."

He pulled her to her feet and took the fingers she was using to please herself into his mouth. Sucking all the juices off them, he hummed with pleasure. Releasing her fingers from his mouth, he said, "Baby, I'm about to make you cum all over this fucking room."

With a smack on her ass, he kissed her and pulled her thong off. "Get on the bed. Spread that shit wide so I can see it. Put my name back on it."

Wasting no time, Taj laid on her back with legs open for Indie to see her flower bloom for her. She cupped her breast in her hands and watched as Indie adored the sight of her. Kneeling down, Indie pushed her legs up and took her folds in his mouth causing Taj to squirm and grip the sheets.

"Damn it, Indie." Her eyes rolled into the back of her head.

Indie didn't let a drop get away from him. He sucked, licked and tongue fucked her and watched as she came undone underneath him. Hooking his arms around her legs to steady her, he could feel her quiver underneath him.

"Oh my ...shit!" she tried to catch her breath, but she couldn't. Every nerve in her body was tingling, her words were getting caught in her throat and she tried to move his hands so she could run.

Indie chuckled against the folds of her pussy, remembering the first time he did this and lost her mind. "Uh huh. Run from me and I won't stop."

"Baby," Taj whined with her legs shaking in his hold.

"Cum for me," Indie managed to say between massaging her pearl with the thickness of his tongue. She hummed and cursed and pushed her head in further unleashing built-up tension into his mouth. Happily drinking every drop, he didn't stop until her orgasm had subdued.

"Give me a minute."

Indie stood up and chuckled. "Baby, I gave you four years."

"I wasn't getting it like this for four years," she replied, looking at him stroke his dick in his hand. The sight of it made her mouth water and her yoni throbbed and got wet all over again.

Indie settled between her thighs and kissed her lips. Taj moaned at the taste of herself. "Mmm, fucking good ain't it?"

Taj sucked his lips while Indigo pushed his dick between her folds. She dug her nails in his back and gasped for air. A flood of emotion took over her. Her eyes fluttered, threatening to spill over. Indie's length and girth, stretched and filled her up and back arched to welcome him home.

Their moans and groans resounded through the room. Her left leg rested on his shoulder while the right hooked around his waist.

"Oh yesssss," Taj hissed into Indie's shoulder. "Right there, baby."

Indie grunted heavily in her ear while their bodies glided over each other. "This pussy is mine. Say it."

"This pussy is yours, Zaddy," her words slurred, and her body gushed. "All fucking yours."

"Good, turn that ass over so I can remind you what it's like to fuck with a real nigga," his voice rumbled seductively, and Taj did exactly what he said. Turning over and propping herself on all fours, she yelped with a mixture of pleasure and pain as he rammed back inside.

Her juice dripped down her thighs. "Yes, yes, yes!"

Gripping the sheets, biting her lip while Indie delivered mind-numbing dick and smacks on the ass which made the tears release and fall on to the sheets. Taj lifted her body so she could reach behind her and hook her arm around Indie's neck and feel his breath on her neck. He reached in front of her and massaged her pearl while he stroked.

"Shit, baby."

Sweat dripped down her chest as she rode him. Her palms laid flat on his chest. She'd lost count of her orgasms; it didn't matter what number she was on as long as he kept them coming like this. She locked eyes with him and rocked back and forth. "I love you."

Indie held it together until those words left her lips. He sat up, wrapped her in his arms as her speed increased and her walls tightened. "I love you more."

Taj wrapped her arms around him. They both reached their climax and exploded. Indie wasn't going to pull out, his seeds sprayed her walls. "You're mine."

Coming down off the orgasm, Indie wiped the tears from her eyes. "You're mine."

Taj dropped to her side and fell asleep the moment her eyes blinked closed. Indie was right behind her.

THE LIGHT FROM THE MORNING SUN CREPT INTO THE room, waking both of them up. Taj's once silk pressed hair was back to its natural state covering her face. Indie glanced down at her and chuckled. "We might need some new sheets."

"And a shower," Taj's groggy voice clashed against his ears. "Call for room service and meet me in the shower."

Tiredly scooting for the bed, she struggled to walk straight to the bathroom. "Damn it."

"I'm not done either."

They didn't leave the room. They spent the day wrapped in each other arms, talking, watching movies, eating and fucking up more sheets. Taj had missed her flight and had almost fifty missed calls from Malcolm.

Indie ignored it and so did she. Eventually, it would die and he would get the picture.

Indie kissed the top of her head and watched the sunset from the balcony of the room. "I missed this shit."

"Sunsets?" Taj played like she didn't know. A giggle escaped hearing Indie huff.

"You know damn well, I meant being wrapped up in your ass all day."

"Me too," she buzzed against his chest. "I haven't had this in years. I missed you so much."

"There wasn't a day I didn't think about you. I had my eye on you until you moved. I went to your apartment after graduation, but you were gone," Indie admitted.

Taj lifted her head and looked at his face. "You were there?"

"I was."

"I could feel you. I cried so much the night before," she mumbled, pressing her lips against his chest.

"I've never been too far away from you, baby. I will never be too far from where you can't feel me."

Taj straddled his lap and tenderly kissed his lips. "Really?"

"Really."

"Mm, then let me feel you again."

Indie smirked devilishly and licked his lips. "Say my name."

"Indigo," she moaned, feeling his fingers inside. "Mm, Indigo"

She bounced her ass up and down, not caring who saw it from the beach. Locking eyes with his she smirked before dropping her head back. "This feels amazing, but I want the dick, Indie."

He pulled his fingers from inside of her and placed them in her mouth as she freed his erect dick and slid down on it. She watched his mouth open and his eyes roll in the back of his head. Taking this time to take control she moaned, "Say my name baby."

"Taj...keeping fucking around and you won't be able to walk."

"That's the point so shut up and fuck me."

"Say please."

"Please, fuck me, Zaddy." She made her request known and Indie delivered. She wasn't going to walk right for a week.

Untitled

'Cause when it all comes crashing down on me
And when the world turn they back, it's up to me
All my flaws and sins, that's all they see
And when it all falls down, it's all on me
It's all on me
Chris Brown: All on Me

Chapter Twenty-Two

I ndigo

HAVING TAJ ALL TO HIMSELF FOR THE LAST TWO DAYS meant more to him than she knew. As the sun made its way over the horizon, he took this moment to admire her sound asleep wedged underneath him. He didn't want this to end but he knew that she had to go back and cut some loose ends and return to work. He'd already let Manny and Rico do whatever they wanted to do for that past two days; he knew that he would have to get back to the business at hand before they managed to fuck something up. But it wouldn't be until he spent the rest of the day with her before taking her back to the airport.

Wrapping his arms around her, he kissed her face and inhaled the scent of her washed hair. A light tap on the door indicated that room service was on the other side with breakfast. Pushing himself up out of the bed he shuffled to the door, opened it and let the concierge in to park the cart against the wall. Indie tipped him and closed the door behind him.

Walking back into the room he looked at the mess that they managed to make. Picking up the pieces of his suit, her dress out the corner, torn underwear, and her engagement ring, he stood up and held it in his hand. He smirked softly and muttered, "Nice try nigga."

Indie placed the ring on the nightstand and put their things in a laundry bag compliments of the hotel. When she passed out the day before from a sex-induced nap, Indie traveled down to his car and grabbed the duffle bag he had in the trunk. He kept it in there in the event he ever had to get out of town easy.

Once he straightened up the room, he crawled under the covers and parted her thighs. Taj hadn't put anything on since she'd been enthralled in his aura. That's how he liked it. Taj completely naked, no image to uphold or people to impress, just her in her rawest form. The warmth between her thighs was pulled into his mouth and she squirmed, coming out of her sleep. The gasp released, her hand on the back of his head, her hoarse voice calling his name, and the sweet taste of her nectar was his pleasure.

He was going to be sure that every step she took she thought about him. Enjoying his first taste of breakfast in the morning, he pulled an orgasm from her and pushed himself up to kiss her lips. "Good morning."

"Good morning," she hummed against his lips, catching him by the dick and hoovering over her opening. "I like being woke up like...thissssss."

Her pleasure induced hiss made him laugh as he plunged inside, making her eyes roll back. "I don't want you to go."

"I don't...I don't either," she buzzed.

That was the last series of words spoken before they

blessed each other with a quick session to keep their minds on each other while they were apart.

Taj was wrapped in the sheets, humming in her afterglow and rocking back and forth eating her eggs, bacon, and toast. Indie ate but watched the happiness seep through her pores. He didn't want to ruin the moment but there was a pressing issue that needed to be discussed.

Taking a bite of bacon, she caught his pensive expression. "Uh oh, what is it?"

"I don't want you to leave but you have to," he rumbled, picking her ring up off the nightstand and handing it over to her. "That loose end has to be tied up. I'm not sharing and I sure as hell don't want to have to push a niggas top back to let him know who the fuck he's dealing with."

Taj rolled her eyes at the thought of Malcolm. She'd been sure not to bring him up at all. Bringing him up meant that she would have to answer questions honestly. It was possible that every question that she answered would send him through the roof.

"I know," she droned, looking at him. "It'll be taken care of the minute I get back."

"I got a feeling that I need to go with you just in case that nigga acts like he doesn't have no fuckin' sense," Indie huffed and ran his hand down his face.

"Baby, I'll be fine. I'll call you when it's handled. Sooner that's over the sooner I can get back to you."

"That's that shit I like to hear but if he looks at you wrong, he's done," Indie warned.

He let the subject go and enjoyed the rest of the morning with her before taking her to the airport. He walked her to her terminal and sat with her until it was time for her to board the flight. Taj wrapped her arms around his waist and kissed his chest.

"You call me if you need me," he mumbled in her ear. Taj looked up at him and nodded with sadness in her eyes. "Hey...I'll see you soon. Let me get some shit in order with these niggas and I'll be there by Friday...okay?"

"Okay. I love you."

"I love you more," Indie kissed her lips as they called her section again. "Go get your ass on that plane before I give these people in here a show."

Taj laughed, slacked his chest and pulled away. "Friday?"

"Friday."

Indie placed his hands in his pocket and watched as she started off to board the plane. Taj looked back once, flashed him a smile before disappearing. Indie didn't move until the plane had taken off. Making his way out of the airport, he headed back to meet with Bobby before heading to Crenshaw to check in on everything. On his way, he called Ricky so they could meet with Manny and Rico. The last bit of product Indie controlled through TK's suppliers was gone and it was time to make the transition.

Lost in his thoughts of Taj and shutting down the operations. He couldn't have planned this shit any better. Everything he wanted was falling into place, now he just needed to get Joey home. Pulling off the highway toward Bobby's office, he hoped to hear some goods. Hopefully, Joey had learned his lesson and was going to be on the straight and narrow when he got out.

Indie walked into his office and greeted the receptionist who escorted him back to Bobby's office. "Indigo Sims!"

"Bobby," Indie greeting him with a smile, handshake, and half hug. "What's going on?"

"I got some good news for you. I just got back from seeing Joey and he's excited. Normally, for this charge people don't get off easily. But it's a damn miracle." Bobby clasped his hands together and looked at Indie.

"Come on, you know I don't like the suspense thing," Indie huffed. "Tell me what's good."

"All the charges have been dropped; the arresting officer seemed to lose all the evidence. But you know the bastards down there at the county, they never let you leave clean."

"Don't I know it," Indie groaned.

"Joey is going to be released soon but he will be on probation. I put you down as the next of kin but there's an issue."

Indie furrowed his brow and twisted his face. "What's the issue?"

"You're under investigation by the LAPD for your involvement in the death of TK," Bobby shared studying Indie's face for any implication. But Indie held his unreadable expression before laughing.

"They won't let it the fuck go, will they?" Indie's chuckle threw Bobby off. "Tell them happy haunting. Joey staying with me won't be an issue."

"Indie is this something I need to worried about?" Bobby asked as Indie stood up to his feet.

"You don't need to be worried until I tell you to be worried," Indie responded. "Ain't nothing. They won't find shit."

Bobby groaned and sat back in his chair and palmed his face. "Did you tie up all the loose ends?"

"There are no ends to find," Indie assured him before turning to walk out his office. "I'll be seeing you."

Pulling up to the spot, he parked his car, killed the engine and hopped out. Locking it and looking at a couple of runners standing outside, he pointed to them and said, "Don't let nothing happen to my shit, nigga!"

"We got you Indie," they spoke up, throwing a nod his way

INDIGO HAZE

before he traveled inside. He was sure to talk to everyone as he walked to the back. Give daps, ask about their day, they're families and whatever else they had going on. Finally reaching the room, Manny, Rico, and Ricky sat around blowing smoke, waiting on his arrival. "You niggas chillin' huh?"

"Waiting on you, cuh," Manny spoke up. "What's going on?"

Indie dapped the three of them before leaning against the desk. "I got an offer for y'all. If you take it bet, I'll be happy with it. If you don't, I completely understand."

Chapter Twenty-Three

Ricky

Ricky sat back in his seat and watched Indie fight to put calmness back in his face. Manny and Rico couldn't pick up on it, but Ricky could. After two days away hemmed up with Taj, he expected him to return with a pep in his step, not looking like his mind was running a mile a minute.

"What you got, Indie?" Rico questioned, looking at him.

Indie looked at Ricky who nodded his head. "Go 'head."

"I'm officially out of product. Y'all can either go legit with me or stay in this shit and be dead in a few years. It's all up to you," Indie spoke up. "Ricky and I got three businesses opening up. We're trying to get all the buildings up to code and we need all the hands on deck we can get. I'll pay you; I'll make sure you and your family are good but you can't be hustling this shit on the side."

Ricky shifted in his seat a little, hoping that Manny didn't say anything about the work Ricky unloaded on him. Cutting his eyes at Manny, Ricky gave him a warning look and Manny caught it. "I got you, cuh."

Indie nodded at Ricky and them looked over at Manny and Rico, "What about you two?"

Manny nodded his head slowly. "I can't believe that's really a question nigga. Look, cuh. You the only nigga out here that's looking out for the same niggas in the hood that grew up with you. Don't nobody else give a fuck about us, about the code, about nothing. I'm following you off a fuckin' cliff."

"I second that shit," Rico spoke up. "Say the word and we go you."

"Aight," Indie nodded. "Y'all take the day off. I got some shit to do. Ricky stay back for a minute."

Manny and Rico dapped up Indie then Ricky before walking out of the house, chatting among themselves. Ricky looked at Indie and raised his brow. "What the fuck is up with you? You should be happy as fuck you got your girl back."

"Yeah, and just as fast as I got her, I might lose her again." Indie shook his head and palmed his face. Sitting on top the desk, he looked down at his feet. "I met with Bobby. The good news is that Joey is coming home in a few days. The bad news, the LAPD is investigating TK's disappearance and my name is at the top of that list."

Ricky groaned. "Oh fuck."

"Oh, fuck is right. You don't think those nigga's left any loose ends, do you?" Indie questioned, looking at Ricky.

He shook his head no. "'Cause if they did, it's their asses too. Nigga's ain't out here trying to get locked up on that charge."

"Exactly," Indie agreed, running his hand down his face.

"Don't stress over that shit, they ain't going find much of

nothing. Especially if Bobby is involved," Ricky assured. "How was your two days in paradise? Y'all are good now?"

Indie let a small smile creep across his face and made the scowl disappear from his face. "It was good actually. Real good. She should be landing any minute now. If she doesn't call me by tonight, I'm going to take my ass up there."

"She calling that sham of an engagement off?"

"I ain't sharing shit. It don't matter how much I love her," Indie grunted.

Ricky chuckled. "I don't think that's going to be a problem. The only nigga who loves his bitch ass, is Senior. He's going to be the only one distraught that she's not marrying him."

"What is that nigga's deal anyway?" Indie questioned as Ricky shrugged his shoulders.

"We will never know. That nigga just different."

Indie rolled his eyes and yawned. "I can't fuck with the thought of him right now. I'm fucking tired."

"Yeah, but we still got to check on the buildings so, let's go. I'm riding with you," Ricky announced, standing to his feet.

Indie followed him out and climbed inside of his car. They headed toward the commercial buildings and for most of the ride, Indie was quiet leaving Ricky to think of creative ways to sell off the rest of his product without Indie knowing.

"You ever thought about how our life would end up if we didn't have any dreams?" Ricky asked, looking out the window.

"We were wild niggas already, but we would probably be dead if we didn't have anything to look forward to," Indie spoke. "You wouldn't be married with a son and I for sure would have been in the ground. Our dreams kept us alive. They gave us hope, fed us when we were hungry and kept the lights on. But look around at what we're doing, how far we've come...we're making it out and we're taking niggas with us."

"This is some heavy shit," Ricky muttered. "Heavy shit."

They pulled up to the commercial complex and checked on everything. Leroy had been hard at work, without anyone having to come to check on him. "Indie!"

"What up, Le!" Indie shouted over at Leroy. "You lookin' good!"

"So are you, like you a got a woman!" Leroy shouted back.

Ricky looked at the way the two interact and how Indie cared for him regardless of what anyone had to say about it. The love Indie gave to everyone was real, he made his stance clear and made sure to reach out to everyone he could. Even with the stress of the investigation lingering, Indie was returning back to himself. Now, Ricky needed to make sure that he held his weight and pulled away from the streets before he couldn't.

Chapter Twenty-Four

T^{aj}

I'M HOME, I'LL CALL YOU IN A FEW. TAJ SENT HER TEXT TO Indie before she put the key in the door and turned the lock. She was hoping that Malcolm kept his word and left. Walking into the house and dropping her bags, she looked at him whip his head around and look her up and down. She let out an exasperated sigh and rolled her eyes.

"Why are you here?" she questioned, putting her purse on the counter. "I was hoping you'd be gone."

"Wow," Malcolm released, standing to his feet. "That's how you talk to me?"

"Malcolm," Taj said simply not wanting to be bothered by his antics. "I'm not in the mood to deal with you."

"You must be in a good fucking mood, seeing as how you didn't answer not one phone call from me and missed your flight. You were with him, weren't you?" Malcolm moved toward her slowly like he was stalking his prey.

"I just told you I'm not in the mood to deal with you. Just get your shit and leave," Taj forced, holding up her hand.

Malcolm scoffed and watched the way she moved around. Her skin glowed, her steps were cautious, and her ring was missing. He knew how she spent her time and it crushed him. To say she didn't feel bad would be a lie. Taj probably would have let him down easy if he hadn't been acting like a manic for the last month.

He snarled, "You fucked him?"

Taj blankly looked at him and yawned. "I'm tired, Malcolm. Leave me alone"

"You did," Malcolm released in shock. "You really feeling yourself huh? Throwing that dry ass pussy to a nigga that don't give a fuck about you."

Taj couldn't help but laugh at Malcolm. "This is pathetic, I'm not doing it."

"Nah... you bold enough to fuck around on me, your bold enough to tell me what the fuck you did. You suck his dick?"

Taj pinned her brows together and looked at the crazed look in his eye. She was prepared to fight him back if she needed to. Even more prepared to be sure that Indie, Ricky, and the rest of the set beat him down if he put his hands on her again.

"Answer me! Did you suck his dick?" Malcolm bellowed.

"Yeah," Taj replied with a smirk on her face. "I did. I rode his dick and his face, and I came...several times more times than I have ever with you. I felt safe and wanted. I didn't have to tiptoe around him. I didn't have to fear that he was going to put his hands on me because of the insecurity of not measuring up. To be honest, I didn't even want to come back here and see you. Malcolm, you make me sick."

Malcolm's nostrils flared and he lunged at her. He held her throat tightly but Taj didn't bat an eye, she looked at him, daring him to do something. "You are an ungrateful bitch. You are cold. All I wanted to do was love you, but you couldn't even give me the courtesy of trying to love me back."

Malcolm squeezed her neck tighter before letting go and slapping her across the face. The slap sparked something up in Taj that nothing could save him from. She started to fight him from the kitchen to the living room, back to the kitchen.

"You're a bitch ass nigga! You have lost your fucking mind putting your hands on me like that. Talking about how I'm ungrateful. You're a fucking piece of shit! Whenever something doesn't go your way, you get ugly. Who wants to love that? Who wants to be with that forever?" Taj shouted at him with tears in her eyes.

She dug in her pocket and launched the ring at him. "I don't want to marry you. I never did. I barely wanted to be with you...but Senior..."

Malcolm chuckled, looking at the diamond ring on the floor. "But Senior what? Say that shit."

"He wanted me too," Taj panted, holding a cleaver in her hand waiting for Malcolm to put his hands on her again. "I was the fool that went along with it."

"You really think, I wanted to stay with someone as fuckin' useless as you? I could have any bitch I wanted but your sweet daddy promised me a cut in your company if I hung around and married you." Malcolm looked at Taj's eyes flutter at the truth. "Oh, don't bitch up now, baby. That nigga promised me millions. I didn't want to marry you either, but I faked it until I made it."

"Get out of my house," Taj pointed to the door. "Get the fuck out my house!"

Malcolm thumbed his nose before collecting the ring off

the floor and spitting at her feet. "You and your bitch ass father wasted my fucking time."

Taj's mouth balled up in anger as hot tears streamed down her face. "Go."

"I'll be back for my things."

"No, you won't," she spoke up. "They'll be on the curb with the rest of the trash."

The minute Malcolm walked out the door, Taj broke down. Not because he put his hands on her. Not because he spewed his hate at her, but because Senior did it again. He managed to manipulate the situation she was supposed to have control over. She couldn't understand why Senior was at the epicenter of her heartbreak every single time. Taj pulled herself together and went into her room to pack her suitcase. She needed to get the hell out of this house and there was no better place to go but to Indie. She would have to finally tell him the truth about Malcolm but at least she would be safe.

Being with Malcolm was a mistake that she was just as much responsible for. She should have left him years ago, but she thought she needed someone around. She subconsciously wanted to please Senior and put a smile back on his face, even if it meant sacrificing hers. Not anymore. Taj wasn't going to please anyone but herself.

Packing up all the clothes she could, she dragged her suitcase to the door. Digging in her purse to retrieve her phone, she texted Maria asking her to schedule and meet the locksmith early in the morning. Then she booked the earliest flight back to L.A. and hailed an Uber.

Next on the list, Senior.

Chapter Twenty-Five

S enior

"So, Maggy," Senior started, laying his menu down on the table. "I have to admit, I haven't done this since my wife passed away."

Maggy smiled warmly at him. "Don't be nervous, it's been a while for me, too. But let's take away all the pretenses and just enjoy ourselves."

"Let's do that," Senior spoke with a smile.

The waitress came back to take their orders and they engaged in some small talk before his phone went off in his pocket. Ignoring it, he hit the button through his pants, only for it to go off again. Looking at Maggy, Senior rumbled, "Let me take this."

"Don't be too long," Maggy replied with a warm smile.

Senior nodded and excused himself for the table and saw Taj's name scroll across the screen.

Stepping outside the restaurant, he answered, "Baby are you okay?"

Taj didn't even let his words make it out of her mouth before she screamed into his eardrum," HOW MANY FUCKING TIMES ARE YOU GOING TO PLAY WITH MY FUCKING LIFE?"

"Whoa calm down!" he roared back at her.

"Don't you even. You told that bitch that he was going to get a stake in my company if he married me? The company that I worked my ass off for? Are you fucking serious right now? What kind of father are you!"

Senior couldn't find the words to say. His chest got tight hearing Taj scream at him with so much hurt in her voice. "Cat got your tongue now? You can't talk? Every time I try to give you a chance, you do something else that makes it really fucking hard to love you!"

"Taj let me explain," Senior managed to say.

"Explain what? Huh? How you played the fuck out of me?" Taj scoffed and her voice broke. "I stayed so I could make you happy. I stayed because I figured if daddy thinks this is good for me it has to be good. But it wasn't good. It was okay in the beginning until he got tired of waiting for me. When he raped me, and put his hands on me, and spit at me. You know what he called me...a useless bitch. The worst part about this dad...you weren't even there to protect me. I keep looking for you to shield my heart from this shit and trying to justify why you let me down but not anymore. Forgiving you is off the table because that was some foul shit. Please do me a favor and stay the fuck out of my business."

Just as fast as the conversation started, it ended and Senior's anger was higher than the guilt he felt. Taj was justified and

Malcolm was out of order. It took him a few minutes to collect himself before he traveled back into the restaurant. Rejoining Maggy at the table he smiled, trying to shake the conversation off but he couldn't. It was eating him up.

"Is everything okay?" Maggy asked.

Senior cleared his throat, "No and I apologize but something has come up with my daughter and I need to handle it."

"Oh, sure," Maggy replied nodding her head quickly. "I understand. We'll get this to go and we'll just try again."

"I need to go now," Senior spoke as the thoughts of Malcolm violating his daughter came to the forefront of his mind. "I will call you when I get back."

"I will be looking forward to it. I hope everything is okay," Maggy shared while Senior left some bills on the table to cover their lunch.

"Me too." Standing to his feet, he walked over to her and kissed the top of her head before he left.

Senior didn't care how much it was going to cost him to get to San Francisco. He was going to catch the first flight and show Malcolm who he really was. He'd suppressed this side of him for decades, but Malcolm's misconduct had woken the beast up from hibernation.

When Senior arrived in the bay area, he went to the first place he figured he would be, his job. Senior approached the reception desk, he forced a smile and said, "Hi, I'm here to see Malcolm Stewart."

The receptionist looked up at him with a weary look. "Uh, Malcolm no longer works for the company. He was escorted off the premises a few days ago. But he just called with his forwarding address for his last check."

Senior gladly took the address she wrote on a sticky note. "Thank you."

Whisking out the office, he went to the address and banged

on the door. He didn't care about the neighbors or anyone passing by. When it came to his daughter, he dropped the ball before and would never do it again.

After minutes of banging on the door, Malcolm opened it and looked him up and down. "I don't know if your precious daughter told you... it's over."

Senior grunted and nodded his head before reaching out and grabbing Malcolm by the throat and pushing him inside the house. "Did you rape my daughter?"

Malcolm's eyes flooded with guilt. "Huh...so you put your hands on her, too?"

Senior didn't need an answer. With Malcolm's shirt crumbled underneath his grip Senior began to beat Malcolm like he stole something. "Fight me back, nigga! You can hit and beat a woman, but you can't fight a man. You pussy!"

Senior continued to beat Malcolm until he was tired. Towering over his limp body, Senior snarled, "Take this ass whipping with you any time you think about putting your hand on any woman. Enjoy your sorry ass life, fool."

Chapter Twenty-Six

I ndigo

Sprawled out across the couch, Indie looked at this empty house. It needed a woman's touch. He thought about how could he finesse Taj into running her business from here and making this house he bought a home. Sitting up, he walked to the kitchen to grab a bottle of water and peeked out the window for the pizza delivery.

"Where are they?" he muttered to himself. "I'm fucking hungry."

Turning his back to go sit back on the couch, the doorbell chimed. "About fucking time. I swear you move out the hood and expect better service and these niggas still are trash."

Indie fussed with himself before pulling the door open and pulling a wad of cash out his pocket. "What's my damage?"

"I'm thinking you can feed me, and then put me to sleep,"

Taj's voice flowed into his ears. Looking up to see Taj standing on his doorstep. "Or you can just look at me like that..."

Indigo's scowl was taken away by a wide smile and he stepped out the way for Taj to walk in. He grabbed her bags and closed the door. "Come here."

"You missed me already?" Taj replied and turned around to embrace him.

"You damn right, I didn't want you to leave in the first place," Indie muttered, pressing his lips against hers. "Everything good?"

Taj nodded her head, not wanting to give him any details until later. "Yeah. It's taken care of. I just want to lay up under you. Is that okay?"

"Hell yeah," Indie grunted, feeling his dick come alive by just looking at her. "Soon as this pizza gets here though. I can't do nothing to you on an empty stomach. You don't let up off a nigga."

Taj smiled and bit her lip. "Only for you."

After a tour around the house, and the pizza delivery, Taj and Indie laid in his bed watching TV. He knew that something was wrong with her. He could feel it. Pulling her close to him, he kissed her cheek and spoke up, "Talk to me, baby."

"I don't want to ruin the mood, Indie."

"You not telling me what's wrong with you is going to ruin the mood. Tell me what's going on," he replied.

Taj took in all the air she could in her lungs before she exhaled and rolled over to her back. Staring at the ceiling, Taj licked her dry lips and said, "Where do you want me to start?"

"At the beginning."

"Well, before I came back for Memorial Day, Malcolm asked me to marry him. I couldn't fix my mouth to say yes but I was settled on the idea of moving on. I didn't want to, but I was going to. When we got back to San Francisco, he started showing me who he was. Putting his hands on me, getting rough...but today," she started to chuckle, thinking about everything she learned about her father. "Today, I found out that my father told him that if he married me, he would get a stake in my company. I am not even mad at Malcolm, he showed me who he was. But Senior? I keep wanting him to prove me wrong and every time he lets me down."

Indie clenched his jaw, trying his best not to blow up. He didn't want to scare her, and he didn't want her to withdraw now that he had her out of her shell. He wrapped his arms around her and pulled her closer. A simple, "I'm sorry." Made her sniffle into his chest.

"All I wanted is for my dad to be my dad, without trying to turn everything into what he wants. Is that too much to ask? All I have is him," Taj sobbed into his chest and he held her tighter.

"You know that's not true. You have me. I got you. Always. I told you I would always protect you. Tonight, we don't have to talk about it. I will let you cry and wipe your snot on my shirt and when you're ready, I'll be there when you want to talk about it."

"Okay," Taj cried.

His heart ached for her. All he could do was hold her tight and let her cry until she ended up drifting off to sleep. Indie was going to have Malcolm touched, it wasn't going to be hard at all. Soon after Taj started to snore lightly into his chest, he drifted off right behind her.

The next morning, he woke up and looked around for her. Placing his hand on her side of the bed, it was warm. She hadn't been gone long. Indie pushed himself off the bed and traveled down the hall to find her. Taj was in the kitchen, pulling trays off food out a brown paper bag.

"Good morning," she hummed, looking up at him. "You

didn't have anything to make breakfast, so I just ordered some via Post Mates. You want to eat?"

"You know I do."

"The food?"

"Mm, mm, you." Indie smiled devilishly and walked toward her. "I want you on my face. Come back to bed."

Taj traced his tattooed torso and admired his walk with a slight limp. She walked around the counter to him, in nothing her bra and panties. Indie grunted at the sight of her. He picked her up and tossed her over his shoulder and walked back to the room. Laying her down on the bed, he laid by her and pulled her on top of his face. Pulling her panties to the side, Indie devoured her. His nails dug in her ass as she rolled her hips over his face. She came in his mouth and pulled herself from the hold of his lips. Straddling his lap with her ass facing him, she freed him from his boxer briefs and slid down on his dick. A moan escaped both of their mouths. Indie watching as her ass bounced up and down on his dick, leaving a milk coating behind after each stroke.

He reached up and grabbed her hair by the root and held her close. He stroked upward ready to spray her walls. She allowed it reaching her peak too. "Ohh Indie, yesssss."

He grunted, letting himself go. She didn't stop bouncing until she milked him dry. "Fuck, girl."

Releasing her from his hold, he kissed her lips. "Damn it, Taj. I love you."

"I love you," she hummed, strutting off into the bathroom to shower.

Indie fell back on the bed and tried to catch his bearings before joining her in the shower. They washed each other and admired one another. Indie could sleep a few more hours but as he stepped out of the shower, the doorbell rang. Wrapping the towel around him, he held one out for Taj.

"Get dressed and meet me in the kitchen," he directed before slipping out of the bathroom, grabbing a pair of basketball shorts and retrieving the door. He pulled the door open and his face lit up, seeing Joey on the other side. Without missing a beat, he pulled his brother into his arms.

"Welcome home nigga!" Indie cheered in his ear before letting him go. "You good?"

"Hell yeah, I'm good. Happy to be out that bitch," Joey cheered in return. "This shit is nice."

"Ain't shit but a house nigga," Indie muttered as Joey's eyes grew large, seeing Taj walk down the hall.

"Jojo?" Taj looked over Indie's shoulder to see him.

"Hey girl," Joey replied with a boyish grin. "I see you couldn't even wait for a nigga to grow up and come get you."

Taj laughed and hugged him. "Are you hungry?"

"Hell yeah, I can eat... You."

Indie punched his arm, "Mind your manners, nigga. I will fuck you up."

"My bad, I got carried away," Joey replied, rubbing his arm.

Taj rolled her eyes at both of them and walked into the kitchen, leaving Joey and Indie in the foyer dapping each other up and silently cheering. "Nigga, that's you now!"

"All me," Indie beamed, watching Taj heat up the tray of food.

"Don't just stare, come eat," Taj hummed with her back turned to them.

"Oh, you know I like them bossy," Joey snickered, flinching and anticipating Indie's slap upside the head. "Ouch."

"I said I'd fuck you up nigga, I meant that."

"My bad, my bad," Joey winced, rubbing his head.

The doorbell rang again. "Who the hell..."

Indie spun around and pulled the door open. He was

expecting to see Ricky or his mother but instead, it was two detectives. "Yeah..."

"Indigo Sims?"

"Who's asking?" Indie replied. "What y'all want?"

"We need you to come down and talk to us," the older detective with salt and pepper hair, spoke up.

Indie started to close the door, but the detective stopped him. "Make this easy for us and just come on."

"Indie?" Taj asked standing behind him, watching the exchange.

"Baby, can you grab me a shirt and a pair of shoes out my closet?" he asked, glancing over his shoulder at her.

Taj nodded and walked down to the room to grab his things and came back. Indie kissed her lips and got fully dressed. "I'll be back. Joey hold it down until I get back."

"I got you," Joey said, nodding his head.

"Indie?" Taj questioned, wanting to know what was going on.

"Baby. I'll be back," Indie finalized and walked out the door with the detectives. He climbed into the back of the car and avoided Taj's confused stare as they pulled off. He silently whispered a prayer that his past hadn't caught up with him.

THE END FOR NOW

I've been here before, say come back down to earth
Just to resist the urge
Still no breaks on this car, live or die, either or, go for broke
Hustle hard, lead it all, on the floor

- Nipsey Hussle: On Tha Floor

Afterword

Someone said that this was a love letter to the hood.

I felt that shit in my gut. This is my dedication, my feelings in the aftermath...my personal lap, my point to prove.

I thank y'all for reading, for staying solid, this was something I needed to get off my chest. The race isn't done yet. I have a wave to make. I have a chip on my shoulder. I have a legacy to build.

Run your race, master your lane, and stay dangerous.

TMC.

Xoxo,

A.P.

Also by Aubreé Pynn

LOVE WILL FOREVER BE CONSISTENT

Thank you for reading! Make sure you check out my catalog:

Dope Boys I&II

Everything is Love

Mistletoe Meltdown

My Love for You

My Love for You, Always

Say He'll Be My Valentine

The Way You Lie

The Way You Lie: The Aftershock

Run from Me

Love Over All

The Game of Love

Love Knockout

Fight for Love

All to Myself

All to Myself: Love, Power, & Respect

Coldest Summer Ever: A Collection of Poetry

Indigo Haze: Thug Love is the Best Love 1-2

Color Me, You

SumWhereOvaRainbows: A Collection of Poetry

Connect with me on my social media:

IG: @aubreepynn

TWITTER: @aubreepynn

Facebook: Aubreé Pynn

Check out my website:

Aubreepynnwrites.wordpress.com

A million words, in a million books, is never thank you enough for your support.

CPSIA information can be obtained
at www.ICGtesting.com
Printed in the USA
LVHW041933211019
634862LV00004B/929/P